D1564805

Friar Tuck's
Tales For The Common Outlaw

Joe Heilman

PAPA PUBLICATIONS

Friar Tuck's
Tales For The Common Outlaw

First edition

Cover design & layout: Chelsea Heilman
Editing: Elizabeth Liskey, Robin Seiple

To the storytelling bookends of my life:

Granny,
To whom, I grant purple permission to see the King!

My children, Lilly and Jed,
May you come to understand one day…

Contents

Introduction

While rummaging through an old, and rather rare, collection of books kept in the attic by a friend and wealthy collector, I stumbled upon the following. There was no date I could attach to it, and my friend informed me that he had no idea he even possessed such a work, nor had he any interest in keeping it.

Being curious, I took it home and found, to my surprise, strange notes and messages written in an outdated code within the margins and in between the various stories. For your convenience I have deciphered it and written it out in a more legible form.

It seems the collection belonged to someone known to us only as "Sparrow" and was compiled by a Limner Jakes. However, the stories are attributed to one Friar Tuck. Whether this is the Friar Tuck of fable, or only an alias, I do not know. More curious is the fact that the stories are modern and some even futuristic. Yet the inscriptions and condition of the book itself are ancient, possibly dating back to the 15th century. Hopefully you can see, as I did, how magical this collection is, and why I have chosen to publish it for your consideration.

Best regards

J.H.

Sparrow,

Our mutual friend has informed me that you have shown interest in certain tales of a curious nature. Since we have never met, please excuse my use of an assumed name. One can never be too careful.

The stories that you now hold have existed for many years but only as whispers in sitting rooms or mumbles in the darker corners of pubs, as the safest place for keeping them has always been the human heart. That they have now come to you in written form is quite rare and, need I say dangerous, as any such previous "books" or collections have all but been banned, burned, or eliminated.

But before going any further, certain things need to be made clear about the man himself and his intentions.

Firstly, you must know that F.T. (dare I spell it out) and I were companions for a time. The tales I've included I overheard while lingering in places that, shall we say, most men of piety avoided.

Nor were such stories always completely understood. It seems that F.T. was given to a rather vivid and innovative mind.

1

His tales, as you will see, take place in random settings, some of which, I dare say, he only saw through a divine imagination as one looking into the future.

Also, never let it be said that he was an outsider to the established church. The truth is that he was once a devoted disciple himself, and a close friend to the business he ultimately tried to enlighten. Needless to say such visions were not greatly appreciated, nor welcomed, but hasn't that always been the case?

Lastly, know this: His deepest desire was for the world to realize that we have all been included in a "Great Embrace." That we have been entwined in something so magnificent, it at once steals your breath and yet relaxes the human spirit the way nothing else can - the reality of God's unearned favor!

Now that you possess these tales keep them safe! See in them a deeper meaning, and if you dare, prayerfully ask, "Could it be true?"

Limner Jakes

Fresh Hot Soup

The sign read *"fresh hot soup."* It was a raw night. Not cold enough to snow, but cold enough to chill to the bone. A light drizzle fell and a harsh wind blew every now and again making the rain move sideways and sting.

He had been trudging for hours, wet foot weary and stomach empty. He had no home, no family, and no money. Cautiously, he pulled open the door that emptied into a spacious dining room. A warm orange glow filled the place. The floor was polished oak, and there was a fire burning in the corner behind glass windows. The lights hanging from the ceiling were turned down low, and the tables were neatly set with polished silver rolled in white linens.

With a small step inside the doorway, he stood there a moment taking in the scene with an uncertain look on his face. Customers occupied about half of the tables, couples mostly. A young lady dressed in black and standing behind a podium nearby startled him. He mumbled a few words and followed her to a small table set for two near the corner. Laying his pack down he sat facing the door. At first, his haggard eyes darted around the room, but then they simply looked down at the table.

Startled, yet again, his head popped up as an attractive woman stood beside his chair and offered him a menu. Meanwhile, a young man came along side of her and poured water into one of the crystal glasses placed there on the table. The man shook his head and declined the menu. He muttered a few words that she smiled at, and then, taking the menu, walked away.

Within minutes the server returned with a tray containing two bowls. One was covered by a napkin while the other had steam rising from it. She carefully lifted each off of the tray and placed them in front of the man. He stared down into the steaming bowl put before him. As soon as she turned her back he grabbed the spoon lying beside it to plunge in. But then he hesitated for one moment more to study his meal. It was a rich brown broth with mounds of beef and vegetables lying in it. The aroma filled his lungs. The steam rising up into his down-turned face soaked into his pores. The spices tickled his nose. Then, gently, he dipped the spoon into the bowl, took it to his mouth, and closed his eyes to savor the taste. Quickly awakened, he hurriedly uncovered the second bowl filled with fresh cut bread and grabbed a slice.

Hunger swelled. He tried to hold back so that no one would notice - so no one would see just how famished he really was. He desperately tried to slowly sip the soup and delicately dip the bread, but it was no use. Faster and faster he plunged the spoon into the bowl. Like an animal he devoured it all.

After thoroughly wiping the mostly empty bowl with his very last piece of bread he leaned back in his chair and closed his eyes. As he sat motionless he could feel the food working its way through him and he knew this would be the end. His stomach, after days of gnawing at him, had finally won out and cost him dearly this time. A mad dash toward the door, if he even got that far, and it would be over.

Still searching the table and bowls for crumbs, his mind wandered back to when he was a child in Sunday school. There he once heard a story about a hungry man who had traded his birthright for a bowl of soup. He couldn't remember the man's name or even how old he was when he heard the tale. But deep inside he knew that no matter how much time and space between he and that man, they were the same. Like so many down through the ages, passion had won the day and the consequences would soon follow.

His server returned and took up the bowls. She flashed a pleasant smile and inquired as to his enjoyment of the meal and if he'd be having any dessert. The man shook his head as politely as he could, and she walked away. He knew she would soon be returning with the bill. How long would he have to make his break? If he fled at once, she would turn and catch him. But if he waited too long she would be back and expect payment.

Within a few moments she disappeared behind the doors leading to the kitchen. Now was his chance. Quickly he grabbed his pack from beneath the table. He scanned the room. Everyone was absorbed in conversation. The wait staff was nowhere to be seen. No one was watching him. No one was looking. He briskly rose from his seat and headed for the door. He reminded himself to walk quickly and not to run, to fix his gaze confidently in front of him and not look over his shoulder.

His escape was only a few feet away as he braced for what he knew would be coming at any moment: the shriek of angry voices behind him, the cruel hands roughly grabbing at him, demanding of him. He shot out his hand, punched the door open, and the next moment he was once more baptized into the stark elements of stinging rain and bitter wind. For a few seconds the wasteland he had been wandering for days seemed like a refuge. But as he broke into a run, with the rain soaking him again and the puddles splashing up into his shoes, his oasis quickly returned to its actual form.

He knew that this was where he truly belonged and wondered how much longer he could continue until his luck would run out. He searched for a place to hide and maybe shelter there for the rest of the night...

Inside, the server emerged only to discover that her patron had vanished. A large man with a shirt and tie, who looked to be the owner of the establishment, followed her out of the kitchen. After first inquiring of the server, he then walked over to the young lady behind the podium and asked her a few questions as well. She shrugged and sheepishly looked toward the door. The man seemed displeased and walked over to the window where a sign hung. Peering out into the night he looked both ways and shook his head. He then pulled up the curtain that had been hanging directly above the sign to reveal the full message that was printed upon it:

FRESH HOT SOUP

Come! All you who have no money
Come buy and eat!
Without money and without cost buy
Wine, milk, bread,
&
Fresh hot soup

God's Falling Light

On a warm summer evening along the boardwalk heaven cleared its throat to speak...

Tourists packed the resort area on vacation from as far away as Vancouver and Wyoming. The smell of the late August ocean breeze and cotton candy wafted about as Friday evening began to get underway. In celebration of yet another glorious summer's end, makeshift stages had been set up every few blocks between the hotels and restaurants. Upon them, the best local bands were invited to perform for the teeming crowds wandering by. Sometimes these bands would bring their own audience, although, the best of them always attracted attention. A well-played familiar tune could catch an unsuspecting ear and cause a passerby to pause for a moment and listen, and quite a few would make an entire evening of it. Often people of every creed and color would bring their picnic baskets and spread their checkered blankets on the grassy lawns next to the boardwalk to enjoy the blues or jazz. Young couples would cuddle close and dream of the future as the music washed over them. Blooming families would watch their little ones run around playfully as overpriced ice cream dripped down their chins. Older couples would bring their lawn chairs, hold hands, and reminisce as they smiled at the children. They might even dance a tune or two if Benny Goodman or Duke Ellington was on the menu for the evening. On this night, however, it was rock and roll.

The band had begun about seven o'clock as the sun was still high and only just beginning to think about setting. They hadn't brought a crowd with them, but they were loud enough that it didn't matter. Whether you loved the music or hated it, the one thing you couldn't do was avoid it as the powerful trio blew through popular songs sure to gain immediate interest.

They were obviously a bar band. The lead singer's voice was lacking at best, but it didn't matter. He made up for it by playing a Gibson Les Paul through a Marshall stack and could mimic the style of almost any great guitar legend. Every song was seasoned with at least a five-minute solo, whether it required one or not. Of course interesting guitar tricks were thrown in for added value, like playing it behind his back or with his teeth. Slowly, a crowd started to gather on the grass in front of the stage. Lawn chairs and blankets began to appear.

Beach towns tend to attract their fair share of home-less people. Maybe they come because the climate is fair or because the police are more lenient than in larger cities. Or perhaps they migrate toward the coast solely in the hope that wealthy tourists might be more inclined to give. Whatever the case for their presence, as the music began to pulse, a small band of wanderers and down-and-outs made their way onto the lawn facing the stage. They clustered together in the back left corner. Some of them had blankets to sit on while a few made use of their backpacks or duffel bags for cushions. Others just sat or sprawled on the lawn. Most barely even noticed them until the end of every song when the loudest applause, cheers, or catcalls would come from deep in the crowd where the ragged people had now gathered.

It was a Buddy Miles song that started the incident. As soon as the band lit into the funk-rock classic "Them Changes," a great shout was heard from the back of the lawn. Within seconds, two homeless men made their way up to the stage and began to dance. No one in the crowd had been dancing to the music yet, especially in front of the stage where there was a large concrete slab for people to do so if they wished. And now that these two had taken over the dance floor, there was little to no chance anyone would be joining them.

The men danced, oblivious to the crowd, lost in private dreams. By the look on their faces, the song had unearthed buried memories, like treasures they toted with them but kept safely hidden most of the time. It was obvious they were drunk - drunk on revelry perhaps - but more than likely stewed on whatever the forty ounce bottles they had left behind on the lawn once contained. There was no ignoring them, although some in the crowd certainly tried. Some just laughed. Others though were definitely made uncomfortable by these obvious vagrants rearing their heads in such a public way. Unfazed, the two continued their drunken ballet.

However, when the two realized that they were now the center of attention they began to show off. They started to prance around and strut like roosters. They even taunted the crowd and made obscene gestures. There was a minor altercation when a young man seated near the front caught one of the men making some rather inappropriate signals to his girlfriend seated beside him. Meanwhile, the other impromptu dancer took off his shirt and began to wave it around his head like he was getting ready to lasso the moon. The band played on while many of the onlookers anxiously awaited the arrival of the police.

Then a curious thing happened. From somewhere in the crowd, a little boy, maybe four-years-old, wandered up to the stage. For a moment he stood transfixed before the performers. Then he laid his head of blond curls on the platform, as if to give the music greater access to his soul. In an instant he became the conduit of rhythm and began to move with the current. Soon he was dancing as only a child can dance: around in a circle, unselfconscious, and free. The child was as unaware of the two homeless men as they were of him. Then the moment dawned - the men had caught the boy's eye. In an instant they were his new friends, his dancing partners. To the dismay of some in the crowd, the moppet began copying the moves the men were doing. When he returned to his own dance, the men started mirroring the steps that the little boy had invented. At one point, they were all jumping around in a circle. It was pure and playful. It was tribal and magnificent.

All eyes were upon them now as their two worlds collided - one awakened to life, the other redeemed by innocence. And as the sun began to set, angelic rays of orange and gold shot through the clouds, illuminating the small band of dancers. A rare few caught the magic, while most remained unaware, as the tribe frolicked under God's falling light.

Surely He Hath Borne Our Griefs

Montgomery Waits clopped down Lexington like he'd been fitted with a pair of ten-pound shoes.

Big as an orange...

"Monty, it's as big as an orange."

Doctors always had a way of saying the worst kind of things in the same tone a normal person would use to talk about the weather. He had never felt it, really - never even knew it had been there all along, growing inside of him like a deadly weed unnoticed in the flowerbed. If he hadn't woken up one morning feeling a bit funny, it would still be living inside of him, undetected - the size of an orange, the seed of death. Most thought fifty-nine was too young to die, except for Monty's nephew, Stevie, who was a pastor. Stevie told him it was important to take the time to reflect on "the scenes of his life." What was that? Wasn't he supposed to be an agent of hope and divine comfort? He might as well have come right out and said, "It's been nice knowing ya uncle Mont! God's apparently pulled your number."

Regardless, today was the day when he would see

the doctor again. They'd talk about options, surgeons, surgery dates, and chemo. Maybe dying would be better. He quickly banished the thought from his head. There was still too much to live for. He was only a few years away from retirement and a few months from seeing his second grandbaby. He'd have to fight.

"Fightin's what I been doin' my whole life anyway," he would often say to himself.

At ten o'clock, he parked his car in the garage on Tenth Avenue and decided to hoof it the rest of the way. The streets were fairly empty. Most people were already at work. He'd taken the day off to see the doctor. His job had become an afterthought. The most important things in his life had dawned on him rather quickly after hearing the news and selling insurance was not one of them.

The weather was growing colder. People had fall jackets and hats on. Steam was rising from the grates in the street.

As he crossed over Terrace Parkway, music greeted him. It was coming from a few blocks down. Normally, he would have raced on by a street performer, but today he thought he'd stop since he had a little time to spare before his appointment. Lately, he'd found himself lingering longer to take note of little things he once ignored.

Monty stood with his hands in his pockets before the old black man. The bluesman had white and gray stubble on his face and a leather cap pulled down tight over his head. A beat-up wooden chair with a red cushion on it was his throne, and his patched coat and dirty brown work pants marked him as having earned the right to sing the blues. His pant leg on the left side had ridden up, exposing the sock and bare leg above his scuffed brown shoe. On his rounded stomach rested a vintage hollow-bodied guitar, tethered to an antique looking amplifier. The guitar case that lay open in front of him looked as worn as he did. It had deep gouges and scuffmarks all over the sides. Fragments of ancient bumper stickers littered the frame, undoubtedly holding the decrepit case together. Monty stared down into its dirty velvet lining and counted $1.68.

The old man rocked back and forth as he sang. It was a low rumble moan - the sound coffee left too long in the pot would make if it had a voice. Monty hadn't heard the blues in years. He didn't care much for music and mostly listened to talk radio in the car, but he closed his eyes and let the bluesman's words wash over him:

Woman, don't wanna leave ya, bu' Jesus callin' my name
Said baby don't wanna leave ya, bu' Jesus callin' my name
They say the streets is paved with gold in that yonder land

The lyrics stung. He and Nancy had been married almost thirty-five years. Of those years, some of the sweetest had been the last few with the kids gone and the grandbabies arriving. He thought of their first date, their wedding day, the struggles they had come through together, and began to well up with tears.

Child don't wanna leave ya, angel band cross Jordan shore
Child don't wanna leave ya, angel band cross Jordan shore
I hear em' callin' me tonight, home to Jesus evermore

"Not fair, just not fair..." Monty whispered to himself.

It seemed his head and heart had been wrestling lately. His head told him he was lucky to have lived as long as he had, but his heart told him it just couldn't be his time yet. He was almost blubbering as tears and snot began to flow. He had become accustomed to it. He'd been doing a lot of crying in his private moments when Nancy wasn't around. He looked into the old man's eyes. They were deep brown sad, bloodshot, and true.

Monty couldn't stand it any longer. Too much wallowing in self-pity wasn't good. That's what Nancy had said.

"Monty you can't wallow in self-pity."

How these bluesmen sang about heartache and loss all the time was beyond him. Taking one last look at the old black man he found that he was staring back at him. For a second, their eyes met. Monty quickly plunged his hand into his pocket. He grabbed whatever he could, tossed the money into the open case, and walked on as the bluesman's song chased him down the street:

Woman, don't wanna leave ya, bu' Jesus callin' my name
Said baby don't wanna leave ya, bu' Jesus callin' my name
He done took all my burdens, now he'll take me just the same

Dr. Lemon's office was located on the third floor of the office building with the glass exterior. Monty entered the waiting room containing a few people quietly reading or watching the television mounted on the wall. He walked to the restroom and splashed water on his face to regain his composure. Then he made his way to the receptionist, gave her his name, and sat down. Within five minutes, a nurse poked her head out of the door that led to the exam area.

"Montgomery Waits?"

He followed her back to Dr. Lemon's private office.

There would be no exam today, just a consult. He reached into his coat pocket to find the list of questions he had written to ask Dr. Lemon, but it was gone. He must have inadvertently thrown it in the guitar case when he went digging for change. No matter. He'd remember the most important questions: What were his chemo options? Should he seek a second opinion? What surgeons would the doctor recommend?

As Monty made his way into the cramped office he found it painted a calming green with tan wainscoting lining the walls. Bookshelves filled with dusty texts towered around him. The huge black desk was cluttered with papers. Underneath the towering stacks of charts, he could see the outline of a desk calendar graffitied with scribbled notes in red and black ink.

His anxiety peaked as he heard Dr. Lemon's voice echo down the hallway.

"Yes, Mrs. Bookman, twice a day for the next two weeks...No, there should be no side effects...Please tell Charlie I said hello."

Within seconds Dr. Lemon came sliding into the room and plopped down into the gigantic leather chair behind his desk.

"Well Monty, I'm embarrassed... As disorganized

as this office may look to you, I've never made a mistake like this in my thirty years of practice. It seems there's been a mix up of the charts. The x-rays we took of you a few weeks ago somehow got mixed in with the charts from the free clinic we hold around the same time."

Sheepishly holding up two identical folders, the doctor continued.

"Somehow Montgomery P. Waits got confused with a Maynard P. Wilson and, well, long story short, you're fine…You don't have cancer!

"Now, I have no idea what may have caused the sensation that first brought you in here, but the x-rays are completely free of anything abnormal. You probably just strained yourself doing yard work."

Monty felt himself exhale like he'd been holding his breath for hours. He could feel his lungs collapse. He was going to live! The doctor's voice became indecipherable chatter - a muffled and full-fledged apology, complete with free examinations for the rest of his life.

For an entire month, Monty had lived with the fear of death. He had counted his every blessing and considered all the things he'd left undone. Now suddenly every dark emotion had vanished, fleeing so quickly that a vague sense of them still lingered like the straps of a backpack carried over a thousand miles, now removed. He smiled.

"Oh, no problem Dr. Lemon…We all make mistakes…No, I understand completely."

There was nothing left but the exchange of pleasantries. Oh the joy of benign pleasantries! Monty was so shocked and elated that he walked right out of the doctor's office without seeing the receptionist to discuss his bill or next checkup. Before long he was back on the street. He breathed the city air. It was composed of hundreds of smells inhaled by millions of people with a billion different problems - problems like the one he had just been released from. His day of dying would come as it would come to all, but it wouldn't be soon, or so he supposed.

He couldn't wait to tell Nancy. They would celebrate in style tonight, maybe even go on out to that little Italian place she had been eager to try. The world came alive again. Colors looked richer and the faces that passed him all seemed friendly.

He walked by the spot where he had stopped to listen to the bluesman sing just an hour ago. The old man was gone. Hardly a trace was left of his street corner stage aside from the wooden chair, propped up against the brick wall. Overjoyed, Monty never noticed the initials scrawled on the back of it that read: M.P.W.

He began to whistle as he crossed the street and politely nodded to the ladies walking past with their shopping bags.

Sparrow,

That you have come this far may mean one of two things: Either you're intrigued and want to read further, or you find yourself an enemy to the ideas contained here and are looking for fuel to add to your hearth fire. Either attitude is acceptable. However, I will assume the former and completely understand if it changes to the latter along the way.

You may be wondering as to F.T.'s origins. Was there a spark that began such an odd journey away from the status quo into the wider open spaces of life? Perhaps a brief tale, between our tales, is in order.

Before F.T. adopted such views and subsequent reputation, he was simply another servant of the religious establishment, dutiful and dry. His true passion, however, was to save "lost souls."

His heart was so moved that one evening he ventured into a place our brother, Jesus, often found himself - the very lion's den that some deemed disreputable and off-limits.

It was a dirty, low-lit tavern. He felt like a stranger there, but he did his best to look the part and ordered a pint to put himself at ease. He had not come to drown his sorrows or find pleasant company, rather he prayed for an opportunity to offer someone the light of life. It was a slow night and most of the day's patrons had already left for home. For a moment, he wondered if he had made a mistake. Fortunately he soon struck up a conversation with a server wiping down the bar. Her name was Merrit and she reminded him of a beautiful portrait left out in the rain.

Her story was what he expected to hear: A sad tale of a once hopeful little girl grown up too fast. And yet...within the darkened room of her history were beams of light streaming through the dusty windows that simply could not be ignored.

She was profoundly convinced of God's acceptance of her. She clearly saw providence and supernatural protection over her at every turn. Her story was riddled by undeniable miracles, angelic visits, and soul-embracing assurances of her inclusion in the divine life.

Simply put, what struck him was that Merrit was already a saint! All that he thought was inaccessible to her, because she had not performed any of the prescribed rituals, she possessed. Without his or her permission, the Divine had already embraced her. And if she was lost, it was only to who she really was, but never to her Heavenly Father who already held her fast.

Here F.T. had come to impart salvation to starving sinners only to find that his Lord had already arrived and fed the thousands. A most unlikely convert was made that evening.

Limner

Raji and The Lawn

Now the angel of the Lord appeared to Raji one afternoon while he was weed-eating his backyard.

"Fear not," said the angel.

Raji in turn achieved a rather unnatural skin tone and sprinted to his shed, slamming the door tightly behind him. Momentarily relieved, he rubbed his eyes and checked his pulse only to discover that the massive creature had materialized there in the shed. The angel had him cornered now behind an expired bag of fertilizer as it spoke yet again.

"Raji, you are to be the Lord's chosen instrument. You and your home will be a sign and a wonder to this generation. Now, here is what the Lord says: 'For forty days and forty nights you shall not cut your front lawn. And I, the Lord, will cause it to grow so that all my children will know of my great power and love.'"

When the angel finished speaking he disappeared.

Raji fainted.

When he awoke, face down amongst a pile of gardening tools, he could only reason that perhaps the summer heat must have caused him to pass out and have such a bizarre dream. Raji went inside, had a cold drink, and relaxed for the rest of the day.

By the next morning, he was feeling much better. With the alarming incident all but forgotten, he walked out of his front door to go to work but was shocked at how quickly the front lawn had grown overnight. He had just cut it the day before, but now it seemed almost taller than when he had first mowed it. Shaking his head, he proceeded on to the office.

When he arrived back home that evening, the lawn was even taller! A cold sweat began to form on his forehead. Could his dream actually have been real? Could the angel have been right? Was the Lord seriously going to do something miraculous in his front yard? He had heard stories of God parting the sea and leading animals two by two into a boat, but was grass a medium that God even worked with?

Raji thought he might be working too hard. The stress was getting to him. To think an angel had actually spoken to him was preposterous. A good stiff drink and a full night's rest was what he needed.

Much like his father before him, Raji prided himself on his beautiful lawn. He had worked tirelessly on it for years so that it would be the best looking yard in the neighborhood. Recently he'd won the "best lawn" award from the community civic league, beating out the Randal family down the street and old man Jamison on the corner. It was quite the milestone. He even threw a huge block party to celebrate his accomplishment. Of course, no one was allowed on the prized lawn, but a good time was still had by all.

So, it stood to reason that when Raji walked out the next morning he was appalled to see his neatly manicured grass now as high as the flowers in the flowerbed. He would have to mow it when he returned from work that night. However, by the following morning, to his shock and horror, the lawn had grown back to the same unacceptable height. And although he spent the day working at the office, he might as well have been on vacation. The only thing he could think was, "Could it be?"

Over the next two weeks, Raji eyed his front yard in fearful astonishment. No other lawn in the entire neighborhood was growing like his. His pristine plot had become, within weeks, the absolute worst looking patch of land in the neighborhood.

By now he knew that any attempt to cut the lawn would be divinely thwarted. It might even make it worse. Furthermore, his habit of turf management was being starved. At times he would walk out to his shed and stare at his mower for hours like an addict going cold turkey.

Something supernatural was going on. Raji could feel it in his bones. Something powerful, unnatural, and downright unbelievable was happening in his front yard.

Of course he tried his best to explain all of this to his wife, Anesh. She was a thoughtful woman and a good wife. He could see the obvious struggle in her eyes when he told her of the angel's visit and the phenomenon now occurring in their midst. On the one hand, this was the man she had loved and trusted for almost twenty years. On the other hand, as a non-practicing Muslim, she was having difficulty putting the pieces together. Raji stopped bringing in the mail and newspapers, hoping the neighbors would be fooled into believing they were on vacation. It didn't work.

By the fourth week of the most unnatural growth of fescue Raji had ever laid eyes on, his front yard looked like a cross between an untouched meadow and the forest it led up to. The grass was up to his shoulders now. It was becoming increasingly difficult to explain any of this to his highly agitated neighbors. It was even more difficult to explain to the civic league, once his greatest ally. They were now leaving threatening notices of potential fines and other "serious actions" if the lawn remained such an "eye sore."

On the thirty-ninth day the grass stood just over six feet high. Motorists, by now, were routinely slowing down or stopping to take pictures. Raji had to creep out of his backyard and down the alley to get to his car. He had recently started parking about a quarter mile away to avoid notice. Through it all, he could only cling to a scrap of hope that somehow God was behind all of this, but how much longer would it be before his neighbors decided to call the Lord's bluff?

When Raji awoke the following morning, he was at peace. He was relieved that whatever God was trying to say was finally complete. Forty days is what the angel had said… forty days for God to show his sign and then it would be over. Soon his yard and his life would be back to normal. As he lay in the quiet of his bedroom he whispered a silent prayer of thanks for whatever the bizarre experience was supposed to teach him. But his morning of inner peace was abruptly shattered as he gingerly stepped out of his front door.

From his point of view, there seemed to be at least twenty people or more standing on the street in front of his house. They looked shocked and were pointing at him. Some people had cameras - others were talking or texting on their cell phones. He slowly turned to look at his lawn hoping for the best, but not quite sure of what he'd see.

Overnight the lawn had somehow transformed itself. Instead of a dense jungle of upright fescue, the grass had now been smashed down. Raji marched out into the street to have a better view and gasped as he looked up the slope of his front yard.

The grass that had grown to such an exorbitant height had miraculously woven itself together to create what can only be described as a huge portrait. A three-dimensional image was covering the whole of the lawn made entirely of grass. It looked as if the grass had even changed color in certain places to add more depth and contrast. Raji had never seen anything like it, nor had anyone else. The images in the portrait were vivid and the characters were so life-like they looked as if they would open their grassy lips and speak at any moment.

He had seen magazines in the grocery store check out line with pictures of various religious icons making cameos occasionally: a statue of the Virgin Mary crying or Buddha appearing in someone's rice. This, however, was altogether different and unmistakably supernatural.

The lawn had become a beautiful mural of something that, at first glance, resembled "The Last Supper" by Leonardo Da Vinci. The figure seated in the middle of the table must have been Jesus Christ. At the bottom of the mural read the words, *"The Wedding Feast of the Lamb."* It was absolutely breathtaking. But as Raji examined the mural more carefully, his heart began to pound even harder.

It was, in fact, Jesus Christ seated in the middle of the table. To the left and right of Jesus were not disciples however, but rather noteworthy and nefarious figures throughout the history of the world. There sat Attila the Hun, Ivan the Terrible, Joseph Stalin, and to his horror, Adolf Hitler at the right hand of Jesus! Every character was immersed in the moment, each and every one laughing and completely caught up in the joy of the feast. The expression on their faces was that of revelry with the Son of God right in the middle of it all! If that was not blasphemous enough, to top it all off, Jesus was laughing and holding a drumstick freshly pulled from a bucket of Kentucky Fried Chicken there on the table.

As Raji took it all in, he heard someone mutter, "How dare you..." Trying to explain would only make the situation worse. He would sound like a complete fool. Gathering himself, he fled back to the safety of the house making sure to lock the front door behind him.

A prisoner in his own home, Raji spent the rest of the day keeping his family calm and peering out of the windows to see how things were developing. By six o'clock that evening, the street was flooded with people pressing in to see the lawn. Police were directing traffic. All three local news stations had been to the scene. The phone rang continuously, but Raji and his family didn't answer.

Within twenty-four hours of the grassy portrait appearing, the lawn was the talk of the world. There was no TV channel or newspaper that did not cover the story. His scandalous front yard was on everybody's lips, including the President's. Although the leader of the free world was worried about how this piece of art would affect international relations, he made it clear that the lawn once more emphasized Raji's first amendment right to express himself.

Around the clock, people lined the street and sidewalk hoping to get a better view of the lawn. The police presence was heavy given the amount of people, many of them unhappy about what they saw. Within three days of its appearance, floodlights had been set up on the street to illuminate the mural day and night. The light kept the children up at night.

It's not easy to offend three major world religions with one sweeping gesture, but somehow Raji's front yard had accomplished just that. By the fourth day, two mail trucks brought ten boxes of cards and letters to his front door. Raji hid behind the door and, with a garden rake, pulled the boxes inside the house so he wouldn't be seen. Most of the mail expressed people's obvious disdain. Some even came complete with threatening pictures of very intimidating looking lawnmowers. After reading about a dozen letters, he took them all out back and burned them.

Finally, by the sixth day, Raji's family became increasingly frantic. Anesh brought him into the bedroom and sat him down on the side of the bed.

"Raji, please go speak to them. People are demanding you talk. I know you cannot explain any of this if you tried. But for God's sake, for *our* sake, Raji, please do something."

She was right. He had to do something. The children were missing school. He was missing work. They couldn't go out or even open their windows. As the man of the house, he had to make all of this chaos go away.

Steeled by his wife's logic, Raji made his way from the bedroom to the front door. As he stepped out onto the porch, flashes of light exploded and a great roar came from the people gathered outside. He was completely unprepared for this. Never had he dreamed of fame or desired it. And now that it was upon him, and for the reason it was upon him, fame had become absolutely terrifying.

Reporters shouted questions at him as he tried to collect himself. He raised his hand to cover his eyes from the glare of the floodlights and the flash of cameras. People took the gesture, however, as Raji finally preparing to speak. A silence fell over the crowd.

As he stood there, watching the world watching him, everything Raji thought he might say completely left his mind. His mouth went dry and his head started to spin. He *had* to say *something*! Maybe humor would lighten the mood.

"Would anyone be liking some chicken?" said Raji with a forced smile. Nobody laughed. There was no response at all. As he stared out into the crowd of confused and angry faces, absolute terror filled him. This was a huge mistake. The angel had never told him to say a word.

Even if his mouth would work again, which was doubtful at this moment, there was simply no way he could explain the most bizarre and spiritual thing he'd ever experienced. There was only one solution he could come up with at that moment: He fled into the house, hurried to the bedroom, dove under the bed, and prayed that God would take him.

Sometime in the night, cowering under the mattresses with the comforter pulled down over him, Raji finally drifted off to sleep. When he awoke the next morning, he was disappointed to be alive. Sunlight filled the room, and a new day had been given in spite of his earnest wish. He reasoned that as crazy as his story was, it had to be told. Like a zombie, oblivious to his family talking in the living room, he lumbered awkwardly toward his front door. Raji flung it open only to discover that the mural was gone. The grass was back to normal.

The finely trimmed lawn had returned. Apparently, the crowds had dispersed sometime in the night when the image finally faded. All that remained were a few workers taking down the last of the floodlights and some scattered trash. An empty bucket of chicken rolled awkwardly down the street, blown by the gentle morning breeze. It was over.

Although the incident with his miraculous lawn was now in the past, many didn't see it that way. Raji attempted to return to a normal life, but it was not to be. His company didn't appreciate his newfound fame or the time it had robbed them of their employee. Within a week of returning to his old job, he was let go without much of an explanation and given two months severance.

Unfortunately, many of the friends and relatives that Raji and Anesh could always count on in the past found their schedules too busy to come over anymore. But the death threats were the final straw.

One afternoon while walking home from school, Raji's daughter was approached by a stranger and handed a note that read, *"You're gonna burn in hell, and we're gonna send you there!"*

Federal authorities soon relocated the family. They were placed in a new town and given new names. Raji found a job at a small department store working for slightly over minimum wage. Even so, it was difficult to make sales when most of the world recognized your face as that "sacrilegious artist who mocked Jesus on his front lawn." He couldn't help but chuckle when he would overhear it…he hadn't drawn a picture since he was five years old. Soon he was relieved of the retail job as well. This time, the department store cited cutbacks as the reason.

Raji spiraled into a deep depression. All he had ever wanted out of life was a loving family, a good job, and a home to make beautiful, but now his children had stopped talking to him. He had no desire to find a job even if there was a place in the world that would hire him. As for the house, Raji had completely given up. Although it was new, he hadn't been out to mow the grass, trim the hedges, or even clean the overflowing gutters that desperately needed it. Mostly, he drifted like a ghost around the house in his pajamas and bedroom slippers, drinking heavily and speaking little.

Once more, the angel of the Lord appeared to Raji one early Saturday morning. After months of despondency, Raji was finally carrying out his plan to hang himself from one of the rafters in his new shed, using his father's old belt. He was just about to kick the step stool out from underneath his feet when the angel appeared before him and said, "Raji! Do not harm yourself! The Lord is greatly pleased with you!"

This time, instead of cowering in fear or running away, Raji decided to vent his frustration. What did he have to lose? Hopefully he would finally get it all out and say just the right thing to prompt God to strike him dead. It was a win-win as far as he was concerned.

Loosening the belt from around his neck and stepping off the stool, Raji approached the angel and said, "You tell your God I am not very pleased with him! He does what I did not ask for at my expense and destroys everything. He is a menace! He has ruined my home, my career, and my family and made me 'the most hated man in the world,' according to the front cover of *News Weekly!* So you can tell your God to go find someone else to be running into the ground, sir! I am done!" Raji stepped back onto the stool and began fiddling with the belt.

The angel replied, "Raji, the Lord has sent me to tell you that you have made Him very proud, and that He will restore what you have so willingly given. You see, Raji, He has a very tender place in His heart for the most hated men in the world."

With a flash, the angel disappeared. Raji stood on his stepstool, clutching the belt tightly in his hands for a very long time. He thought deeply about himself, God, the world, the lawn, and all that had brought him to this place.

About eleven a.m., Raji emerged from his shed. Whether it was thoughts of hope for the future or the revenge his well-being would bring to those who wished him dead, he had decided not to take his own life.

As he walked into his house, Raji looked around at his family, pulled Anesh close to him and kissed her forehead. She had just gotten off of the phone with some new friends they had made in the neighborhood. Then, without a word, he walked out into the sunlight and to the middle of his new lawn. It needed a lot of work. Crab grass and clover covered a third of it. He took a look around and began planning how to make it the best looking yard on the block.

The Morgue Attendant

My name is David, David Roemer. The name's not important. Hell, it's not even worth the mention, save for the role it plays in the story you're about to hear. Fresh out of college, I worked as a morgue attendant at Northwest Hospital in Seattle. Eighteen years flew by. My plan was to become a forensic pathologist, but "morgue attendant" was about all I wanted of that life after seeing some of the things you see in my line of work. You just become numb. So, after I had thoroughly anesthetized myself, I figured I'd just stick with the job. After all, who wants a used up morgue tech? It was a simple job really, and the pay was decent. I was responsible for moving and cleaning the bodies. In some cases, I would assist in the autopsy. The bodies were brought down to the morgue either from the hospital itself or straight from the outside, carried by silent ambulance. The deceased were then brought back to us. We'd photograph the people in whatever clothes they were in, strip them for examination, and check for a cause of death. All of this isn't that important except to say that, once you go numb, very little bothers you anymore. You build a wall against distracting emotions. At least that's what I always thought about myself.

I worked the graveyard shift. Feel free to laugh at the irony. Eleven to seven. One night, I had come in a bit late. It looked slow. Not too much was going on. I remember it was raining harder than usual outside. As I went past check-in, Sandy shot me a quick glance as she was talking on the phone. I hurried back into the scrub room to get ready for the night and don my "stiff" clothes. As I was finishing up, Eric, the three to eleven guy, came in and said, "Where you been Roemer? You missed all the excitement! Come here. You need to take a look at this." I always thought Eric was a bit of a nuisance, but his enthusiasm intrigued me so I played along. We walked into the exam room.

Laid out on the table was what looked to be a male in his mid-to-early thirties. His skin was dark, not black - maybe Hispanic, American Indian or Middle Eastern. I wasn't sure. He had a shaved head and very little body hair. So far, it sounds routine, right? Well, that's where it stopped. Now, don't get me wrong, I'm a fan of body art. I've always dug a cool tattoo, but this guy was covered with them. And when I say covered I mean *covered*. Every inch of his body had ink, even the bottoms of his feet. I didn't know what to make of it. Maybe he was part of some weird cult, or an Indian. Or maybe he was just what I figured - a freak. He was probably one of those troubled sorts who never quite latches on to responsibility and winds up on the fringes of society. What's the phrase? "Live fast, die young and leave a beautiful corpse?" Well, I don't know about beautiful, but I will say it was original.

From the looks of him, he went out quick. He had taken a few bullets to the chest. I picked up his chart dangling on the end of the table and scanned it for the pertinent information.

> John Doe
> Age: Unknown
> Sex: Male
> Race: Hispanic
> Cause of Death: Five entry wounds to the chest. Close range. 45 magnum.
> No exit wounds.

No exit wounds?

Eric said something like, "Ain't that the craziest thing you ever seen?" as he walked out leaving me with the tattooed dead man.

As I looked at the body, I couldn't help but marvel at the artwork. There were no pictures of doves, or skulls, or the name of some girl he promised his heart to in high school. Just wild swirling patterns like tribal bands from head to toe. I was left to bag and store him until we were told where and when the body needed to be moved.

After putting John Doe to bed, I walked back to the check-in room to chat up Sandy.

"What's the deal with our damaged piece of art in there?" I asked.

Sandy told me it was a homicide and that the cops had found him in the park down around Third Avenue. I knew the area. It's one of those places you didn't want to be after dark. There had been a lot of drug-related violence happening down there for a while. The police were always bringing by the latest casualty.

I finished my shift at seven, stopped to get a bite to eat, and went home to hit the sack. It was my routine, six days a week. Not much of a life, I know.

Now look, I'm not one for dreaming. Typically, I'm so exhausted from slinging dead weight around that I sleep like one of our clients, but this morning was different. My subconscious must have started spinning like a hamster's wheel as soon as I hit the pillow. And guess what kept coming up? That dude from the morgue, "Mr. Tattoo guy." The more I dreamt of him, the more the dreams rattled me. I woke up about three o'clock in the afternoon and decided to go for a drive. I couldn't get him out of my head. I guess what got to me was the way he looked in the dreams - not riddled with bullet holes, but full of life and energy. In one dream, he'd be laughing and swinging a little girl around in his arms. In another, he'd be sitting beside me at a Mariners game or walking by me on a crowded sidewalk, his face on everyone I passed. The more I dreamt, the more bizarre the dreams became. The craziest thing was the color of his eyes, like the sky on a clear afternoon. Since sleeping was no longer an option, I found myself driving down around Third Avenue.

I figured the crime scene was probably still marked from the night before. Sandy had mentioned something about a park. A wild guess turned me on to a small plot of grass in the middle of the worst looking projects Seattle had to offer. Adjacent to it was a dilapidated playground and a basketball court surrounded by a rusty fence. I pulled into the small parking lot and got out of my car. It looked pretty deserted, but I imagined it became a hot bed for drugs and prostitution after dark. Carefully walking across the soggy grass, and occasionally looking over my shoulder, I spotted where the murder must have taken place. The cautionary yellow tape was still draped on makeshift poles. I wandered over to the scene and noticed a girl sitting in the middle of the marked-off square. She was sitting cross-legged in the middle of a crime scene, crying, and holding a dandelion. I just stood and stared. Eventually, she looked up at me and didn't seem to be offended in the least that I was gawking at her pain. I spoke as gently as I could.

"You know, you probably shouldn't be in there. More than likely the police will be back soon to finish their investigation."

She looked at me with the eyes of a lost, little girl and said, "Did you know Baba?"

I assumed she meant the corpse I had wrestled with the previous night. I said that I didn't know him, but that I had helped with his body.

"My name is Spring. You know he was a healer, right?" she said, lightening up a bit.

"Excuse me?" I said. "A healer? Um, no I didn't know that."

I assumed she must have been smoking some of that stuff Baba got killed for the night before.

"You don't believe me do you?"

Trying to avoid an argument, I responded that I

didn't know him or how he died, so I couldn't really say *what* he was.

"He died protecting me," she said. "I used to work these streets for Pretty X, the biggest dealer around here. A couple of years ago, I ran away and came here to make it on my own. That's when I met Pretty. He said he'd take care of me, but he just got me all strung out on smack and put me out to work…said I needed to earn my keep. That's when I met Baba. He saw me working the corner one night and brought me back to his place for a hot meal and a shower. He sort of freaked me out at first, but he was the kindest person I ever met. He didn't even touch me except to hug me and kiss my cheek. Baba was special, maybe 'divine' in a way. After awhile he began to come around more often, always helping me with money or food. Mostly it was his words that healed me…but, he *did* heal me.

"One night, a few weeks ago, I was in real bad shape about two blocks from here. Baba found me in an alley, OD'ed. He bent down, put his hands on my head, looked into my eyes and asked me if I wanted to get clean. I guess I said that I did, so he said, 'Be clean,' and I was. It was like a second after he spoke the words, I could feel the poison in my veins turn into vapor and disappear. My head got clearer than it had been since I first left home. I walked out of that alley and I never went back to Pretty for more junk. That *really* made him mad.

"So last night, I went to Pretty's place and tried to explain what had happened to me. I thought maybe he would leave me alone if I could make him understand that

I didn't need his help anymore. Instead, he was furious and started throwing me around. I knew things were gonna get crazier, so I bolted. He started chasing me with a gun, screaming about how he was gonna kill me and how I'd regret ever walking out on him. So I ran to the park, hoping someone would help, but there was nobody around. I couldn't run anymore. I turned around and Pretty was ten feet behind me. I figured that was it.

"That's when Baba showed up. I never saw him until the last second. Baba jumped in front of me just as Pretty pulled the trigger. I guess he thought if he unloaded enough bullets, one might sneak its way through Baba and into me. They didn't. Pretty ran away after the last bullet. Baba and I crumbled to the ground. I could hear the sirens coming but Baba was already gone. I was so dazed I just kissed him on the forehead and ran away, but now..."

She couldn't talk anymore as the tears began to well up in her eyes.

I asked if there was anything I could do for her, but she said no. She said that Baba had taught her how to live and that she would be all right now that he had shown her her name.

"Shown you your name?"

"Yeah, my name..." she said, like I had missed something obvious. "Didn't you see it last night? The tattoos?"

"I'm sorry...I haven't had a lot of sleep. I'm not following you."

Then she said, "Baba has every person's name

42

written on his body somewhere. It's what makes up the pattern."

"He has everyone's name written on his body?" I repeated with some obvious doubt in my voice.

"Yep. I'm written on his left shoulder. If you go look you'll find yours too."

Ok, I had heard some weird stuff in my life, but that was the weirdest. I told her thanks, but no thanks and left her there. Poor girl. I'm glad she found comfort somewhere in this world. It was almost time for my shift, so I cruised into work a bit early.

Curiosity is a strange thing. It will make a man do things that go against all logic. As I walked into work, I saw Sandy back at the front desk. It looked like another slow night. Apparently, Eric had gone home early after complaining of stomach cramps.

"Sandy, do you still have that Polaroid camera back there?" I asked.

Bored, and a little curious as well, Sandy followed me back to the locker. I remembered exactly where I had put Baba. I pulled the drawer open and had Sandy help me get the body to the exam table. She was nervous.

"If we get caught with this body out we'll both get fired!" she said in a shaky whisper.

I told her I'd be quick and started unzipping the bag.

There he was, the patron saint of Third Avenue, giver of hope to the downtrodden, and healer of crack addicts. More than likely though, he was just some tattooed whack job, now a dead guy who had whores believing everyone's name was written somewhere on his body. They were tattoos, just tattoos... Then I noticed something like little breaks in the fibers of the twisted pattern on his skin. I asked Sandy if she wouldn't mind handing me a magnifying glass. I took it from her and held it over Baba's body.

There, making up what looked to be ordinary tattoos, were actually very tiny, unnoticeable to the naked eye, letters. I almost dropped the glass.

"What's the problem?" Sandy whispered.

I said it was nothing and asked if she would go get me something from the snack machine upstairs. As she rounded the corner and headed off, I bent in closer for a better look through the glass. I began to break into a cold sweat.

Names. Not just random letters, names: Jennifer Corbit, Robert Baines, Mufar Quadi. On and on and on they went - letters spaced so close together, no one would ever notice them unless they got as close to him as the clothes he wore. There were thousands of perfectly spaced distinct names, maybe even hundreds of thousands. At that moment, I heard Spring's voice in my head.

If you look, you'll find yours too...

As crazy as it sounds, I admit that I searched and searched all over that dead man's body, but I couldn't find my name. Sandy would be returning soon with my Snickers bar so I quickly proceeded to put Baba back in the body bag. The job was almost complete when his right arm slipped out. Don't ask me why, but a final wave of curiosity came over me. I grabbed the magnifying glass one more time and turned his palm over. Bailey Stevens,

Fredrick Pucko, David Roemer... David Roemer. He had my name tattooed on his hand.

Fumbling for the Polaroid that Sandy had left behind I took a quick picture of the magnified image of my name. Then, the sheer weight of the moment hit me and I dropped to the floor on my knees. The shakes and sweats started taking over and my ears were ringing like I was about to faint. What happened next, I can only explain as the paranormal.

I felt a cold breeze blow by me, and I heard what sounded like breaking glass. I stood up and what I saw... what I saw was - *nothing*. He was gone. He was gone and the bag was empty. He had vanished, leaving only his plastic death shroud. I screamed. Thank God no one was around to hear me.

Dead is dead. Dead people don't just vanish. And I was the only one in the room. How in the world was I going to explain this? No one would ever believe the body, which I unlawfully pulled out of the drawer, with my fingerprints on it, just got up and walked away! I didn't know what to do. I blindly ran for the door, and all I could hear in my head were the words of Spring:

Baba is special... Divine in a way... Baba healed me... Once I saw my name I knew it would be all right.

I hopped in my car and raced for the park. It was dark and probably dangerous by this time of night, but I didn't care. Getting fired for leaving work was the least of my worries. The only thing I could think of was finding Spring.

Arriving at the park, I jumped out of the car and

didn't even bother to turn off the headlights. I sprinted to the place where Spring was sitting that afternoon. As I ran toward the crime scene, I could see two people standing in the square of tape. Right about then is when I tripped and fell over a root. I banged up my knee pretty good but the adrenaline kept me moving. When I hopped back up off the ground, just one figure remained, silhouetted in the moonlight. It was Spring. She smiled at me as I came to her.

"You'll never believe what just happened!" I panted.

"It was Baba, wasn't it?" she said, smiling as if she were relieved to know I finally understood the punch line to a very clever joke.

As I told her about what happened she just stood there and kept smiling at me. She said, "He's alive you know."

"Spring, what is going on here?"

"He told me to give this to you," she said.

From her pocket, she produced a folded piece of notebook paper. I unfolded it and looked at two words written in the same script that covered Baba's body. It read:

Follow me

"What in the world is this? Why does that guy have my name written on him? Who was he? Who is he? Spring, I need you to give me some answers!"

"I can't," she said. "But I'll bet he can..."

Spring pointed to a street light about a hundred yards away. There, in the light, I could make out a figure with a shaved head and baggy clothes. I yelled and chased after him, but he disappeared into the night. I lost him.

When I came back to the park, Spring was gone as well. I never saw her again.

Well, that brings me here...

I know I'm a long way from Seattle. I can't begin to recall the miles I've traveled or the months I've spent searching for him. I've combed the streets of almost every major city looking for the face that haunts my dreams. He leaves behind a trail of healings and altered lives. Every time I feel he's right around the corner, he slips away again. I just can't seem to get close enough.

He goes by the name Baba. You wouldn't forget him if you ever saw him. He's got tattoos all over his body. I've got a blurry picture of his hand if that's any help. He's got my name written on it and I need to know why. He's probably got yours on there too...

Sparrow,

Still at it, I see. Good for you! Never be afraid to be stretched, to be challenged.

Parables are sneaky things, you know. Left to do their work they help us grasp the more subtle realities dancing just under the surface of life. Ideas full of truth, we may have even rejected before, suddenly have an opportunity to be birthed in us.

As for F.T.'s stories some people never got it, never really understood what he was saying. But for those who got it, his parables remain most enlightening and challenging tools.

Of course, he didn't make the leap from dutiful religionist to outlawed storyteller in a night. His encounter with Merrit was only an early clue that something much more sublime was at work in the universe. But it was certainly a start.

You could say her living parable became to him an enigma that wouldn't go away; a riddle that demanded to be unraveled. It kept him awake. It made him uncomfortable at meetings. And as he continued to search for clues of this ever-present, all encompassing love and acceptance he began to see it everywhere.

The scriptures took on a new light. Words once ignored suddenly jumped off the page. The world he thought he had neatly partitioned off suddenly saw its walls crumbling down. If a word could describe what was happening to him it would be: revolution.

At first blush, revolution is a very exciting idea. But what it really means is that there is a desperate bloody battle soon to ensue...

Press on, friend

L.

Captain Ultra:
Beginnings & Endings

A frozen sunrise was breaking on the Arctic Circle as Captain Ultra jolted awake from a dream. He was once again battling his archenemy, Nerofame, in what was more of a nightmare. Like so many of his dreams lately, he could feel himself falling out of the sky - his ability to fly stripped by a blast from Nerofame's thermo-gun. Now, as he lay still in the quiet warmth of the Fortress of Solace, far removed from the citizens he protected, a calm once again washed over him. He realized his dream was simply the product of a wild imagination and a full night of work.

It had been quite the evening. Troubles on the other side of the globe had him calling upon all of his powers to quell the threat to the planet and restore peace and order to a frightened populace. There was no doubt Nerofame was somehow behind the incident, but all was well as Captain Ultra relaxed for just a few more moments before starting yet another hectic day.

Somewhere in the back of his mind was a strange insistence that today was special in some way, but he couldn't quite recall why. No doubt, he'd soon remember what he had forgotten as he went about his morning ritual of scanning the global news and checking with various informants.

As he swung himself out of bed, lifting his head to look out over the interior of his massive bedroom, three alien figures stood directly in front of him. They loomed over him, each one eight feet tall with blue translucent skin and oddly shaped heads. The Fortress of Solace was completely secret and impenetrable. It would take a genius to even find it. Captain Ultra's first reflex was to fire on the intruders with the laser beams from his hands, but as he stretched out his arms to aim, his lasers flickered and died. The aliens had rendered him powerless. He could feel it in his body: his x-ray vision, his superhuman strength, and his ability to fly had been reduced to nothing. His powers had been abducted, as if gently lifted off of him like a light blanket while he slept.

"Greetings Ian Marcus Stewart III, born earth day February 21, 1970. We mean you no harm. We come in peace and for your benefit."

The aliens spoke together as one; all three voices blending to create a beautiful texture of harmony, like a mass choir or large symphony in perfect tune.

Suddenly he realized why today was important. It was his birthday, February 21st. Being a super hero, Captain Ultra had never celebrated his own birthday. Quite frankly, he had forgotten all about birthdays once his extraordinary powers began to manifest themselves when he was just a boy of ten. He would be forty today. These aliens were either someone's twisted idea of a birthday gift or a sinister plan to erase the world's only saving hope. He longed for it to be another nightmare, but the three figures standing in front of him were undeniably real.

"Who are you? What have you done to me? Where are my powers?" Captain Ultra said in his unrattled super-hero fashion.

"Ian Marcus Stewart, today is your reclamation day. We are from the planet Filanthropia. We have come to reclaim the powers that have been given to you as an act of universal kindness in a study conducted by our greatest researchers. Your thirty years are now complete. We must return to our planet with our powers to be analyzed and redistributed."

Captain Ultra's serene exterior began to show cracks.

"What do you mean *your* powers? Those are *my* abilities!" he shouted.

The aliens seemed genuinely baffled by his response.

"Ian Marcus Stewart, how odd of you to think so. The abilities you have enjoyed these past thirty years are simply traits of all the inhabitants of our planet. Thirty years ago, our researchers thought it to be worthwhile to implant our abilities in a lesser species to discover if life on your planet could be improved. You were then selected, from earth's three billion inhabitants, to be the one and only test case. Our experiment stage is now complete. The time has come for us to reclaim that which we have shared with you. We hope you will find your new life as a normal human being again to be fulfilling."

"But this can't be!" exclaimed Captain Ultra. "You don't understand! I'm Captain Ultra! Countless times I've rescued this planet from destruction. I'm their only hope. They need me. Nerofame is still out there on the loose!"

The aliens continued on as if he had never spoken:

"You will find adequate earth currency and clothing to help you once again begin your ordinary earthly existence. You'll need a place to live, as this dwelling will cease to exist once you leave. As for the rest of the inhabitants of this planet you so love, we suggest you not overburden yourself too much with care. We have been observing your world for quite some time and believe it to be stable enough without your intervention. May you find peace in your new life."

With a blinding flash of light, the three were gone.

Captain Ultra sat numbly on the edge of his bed. The absence of his powers seemed to pale by comparison to the feelings that swelled inside of him. How could this be? How could he have been such a fool? The powers that he alone wielded with the greatest ease of justice, strength, and civic-minded duty had never been his at all. Now all of these shared abilities were gone. Everything he had ever known for the past thirty years swept away in the span of two minutes. He staggered to the bathroom as he felt a knot in his stomach begin to tighten. He vomited into the sink and looked at his face in the mirror. Lines, held off by superhuman DNA, now appeared around his eyes. The cheekbones that had once been muscular and well-defined sunk deep into his skin. Small grey patches appeared near his temples. His limbs felt weak. He collapsed to the floor.

The boy was sitting at the breakfast table finishing his morning cereal and toast. His mother was washing dishes at the sink. Papa had already left for work. The burglars appeared in the doorway of the kitchen just as she turned around and screamed - one was wielding a knife and the other a gun. But the boy moved so quickly they had no time to react. He twirled like a cyclone toward the two thieves. The child grabbed the knife, but his other hand just missed the gun. It went off with an earsplitting bang in the burglar's hand. The two men, the boy and the woman stood like statues for a moment as a blood stain appeared through his mother's apron, slowly soaking the white cloth. The men fled through the back door. The boy stood holding the knife, still staring at the crumpled ball on the floor that was once his mother. He rushed to her side, although he had no idea of what to do other than hold her and plead for her to stay. But she was already gone. Then and there he swore he would never let it happen again. He vowed to protect the innocent from the takers of the world. He would live to avenge her loss and stand as guardian of all.

When he awoke, lying awkwardly on the bathroom floor, Captain Ultra was immediately overcome with the shock and anger that haunt the first waking moments of lives stricken by tragedy. He rose gingerly and walked into his bedroom to find a large suitcase containing blue jeans, a flannel shirt, a thick winter coat, shoes, and enough cash to last quite awhile. He proceeded to change slowly into the strange attire of those he had so long helped and protected.

He did not stop to take a last look around the fortress where he had found comfort and peace for most of his life. Rather, like a death row inmate resigned to his sure fate, he slowly marched toward the front gates of his fleeting oasis. He emerged into the frigid arctic air. The sun reflecting off the snow instantly blinded him. The cold took his breath away. So this is what it felt like to be normal, to be like everyone else: cold, blind, weak...

As he trudged through the snow, fighting the lashing wind, he did not look back as the Fortress of Solace crumbled to the ground.

Captain Ultra: Snow

For countless miles, Captain Ultra staggered southward through the snow. Sheer will, mixed with reckless disregard for his own life, sustained him. He slept under overpasses and kept out of the public eye. Within weeks his beard had grown out. Now that the most recognizable face in the world could be hidden, he began to hitchhike. Hitchhiking helped him remember his name: Ian, Ian Stewart. He'd stumbled over the words when the first few truck drivers along Route Twenty-Five asked him for a name. The first time the aliens had said it was the first time he'd heard it spoken in many years. Now he was headed to see the only other person on earth who knew that name - the only person who might understand and help him find some reason to live again.

Meeting Fawn had been nothing more than mere happenstance. Three years prior, on a routine night of patrolling the city of Everchance, she had been just another nameless face in another random hostage situation. He had whisked her away just in the nick of time before the bomb had gone off. He didn't even notice her face until he had flown her miles from harm. As he deposited her on top of the Wright building, she grabbed his arm and whispered, "Thank you" along with, "I never knew super-heroes could have B.O." Well, it wasn't the most romantic beginning, but it was a beginning...

Within a few months, the fiery twenty-four-year-old blogger had somehow extracted more information from Captain Ultra than anyone had ever known. She was tenacious in her pursuit to uproot the details and get "behind the mask." It certainly helped that she had an almost unnatural innocent beauty about her as well. Within months of finding a place in his heart, she had begun her blog. It detailed his exploits as well as some of the lesser-known facts about Captain Ultra. She hadn't asked his permission to do it - she knew he would have said no. Oddly, the blog was something never mentioned between them. She always had a million questions and a flirtatious way of getting her answers. He held back as much information as possible and would often send her on wild goose chases just to keep her safe and anonymous. The give-and-take, or the lack thereof, was what kept the tension in the dance between them alive. Now it was up to Fawn to keep *him* alive, literally.

He had called from a pay phone just a few miles away. Immediately she could perceive a change in his voice. Something drastic had happened to him - as if the hero on the other end of the phone had become frail and weak.

They arranged to meet at Old Times Remembered Diner on Fifty- Eighth. She worked there as a server. Fawn's secret identity as the hottest blogger on the net didn't quite pay the bills. It was her day off, but she agreed to meet him at nine-thirty a.m. The breakfast crowd would soon be leaving, and it would be a few hours before the lunch rush began. They met in their usual booth situated between the end of the counter and the old jukebox that never worked.

As he explained what had happened she listened quietly, asking questions but taking no notes. At one point she ran to the ladies' room to gather herself. It was hard to see him so broken, his hair unkempt and his beard long and full. She hardly recognized him at first, but she knew those eyes. No one could ever deny those steel-blue sparkling eyes.

All she wanted to do was make him feel better. But what could she say? It was hard enough to find words of comfort for someone who had lost a job or even a loved one. How would she comfort someone whose job it was to look after the billions of lives on the planet? He had lost the only life he'd ever known.

When the conversation turned slow, Fawn went all in.

"So Ian, what have you always wanted to do?"

"Do? What do you mean *do*?" he replied.

"I mean aside from saving the planet day after day…" a touch of her natural sarcasm peeking out. "Is there anything you've always wanted to do besides that? A secret dream? A goal? A bucket list? A hidden talent perhaps?"

"Fawn, all I've ever known is saving lives and being a hero…There's been nothing else,"

"Oh, come on!" she insisted. "You mean to tell me there has never been anything else you were good at or wanted to do? You know, after a long hard day of thankless hero work when nobody acknowledged your efforts and the bad guy got away, did you ever secretly wish to trade places with someone, or just be a regular guy?" She was digging now like a good reporter when they sense something just beneath the surface about to emerge.

"Cooking," he mumbled.

"What was that?"

"COOKING!" he looked around embarrassed.

"Believe it or not," Ian continued, "my mother was a chef in a five-star restaurant when I was a kid. She taught me all her tricks and secrets. By the time I was ten I could whip up a glazed duck or a crab-and-spinach quiche at the drop of a hat."

He smiled. It was a grin of fond remembrance.

"It's sort of funny now, but even when I was in my glory days and saving the world, I often dreamed of being in the kitchen instead. As a matter of fact, there were times I'd be right in the middle of a fierce battle with Nerofame, and all I could think about was how long it would take to finish him off so I could fly back to the Fortress of Solace and try a new dish I had dreamed up. Crazy, I know…"

"No! Not crazy at all! Very cool!" she said. She could sense a spark in him now - a twinkle in the eye perhaps. The spark, however, quickly faded.

"Ah… glazed duck never saved the world, Fawn." The clouds came back.

"Well, you never know. I mean, served with the right wine…" she smiled. He half frowned.

"Bad joke, sorry. The point is, *Ian*, now you can do

what you always dreamed of doing! There's no unspoken duty to be something you aren't. Sure you were granted super human abilities. But that didn't mean…"

She was cut off by a news flash on the TV screen a few feet from their heads. It showed dramatic pictures of a battle having taken place in some remote part of the world. As Captain Ultra watched with human eyes, Fawn could see the anxiety spread across his face. It was quickly replaced with sorrow. He could do nothing.

She took his hands in hers to gain his attention again.

"The point is, Ian…the point is… the weight of the world is no longer on your shoulders! Look, if these aliens that took your abilities are as wise and powerful as you say they are, then why not take their word for it and believe them when they told you things will be ok?"

At that moment, as if to drive home the point she had just made, Fawn reached to turn up the TV in time to hear the news anchor conclude:

"…The threat has been defused by the local authorities. Ironically, as the world wonders where Captain Ultra may be, its first major incident without him has been dealt with successfully…"

A look of hurt and confusion crossed Ian's face. But, as he sat quietly for a moment, a sly smile curled the corners of his mouth. He breathed a long sigh of relief. He looked up, sheepishly, like a little boy who just jumped off the diving board for the first time, only to realize that his father was waiting in the water to catch him all along.

"Thank you, Fawn."

The words felt strange coming from his mouth. They were words he rarely uttered in all of his forty years.

"You're welcome, Ian. So... dinner tonight! My place. Be there at seven. You're cooking!"

"Wait a minute. Isn't it rude to invite a guest to a dinner that *they're* supposed to cook?" he said playfully.

It was good to see him smile. Fawn was surprised to notice a significant difference from his Captain Ultra smile. Ian Stewart's smile was a genuine grin of gentle humility. It looked good on him.

Encouraged that the clouds had finally lifted, Fawn replied, "No, not at all. Someone had better try your cooking chops out before you unleash yourself upon un-suspecting citizens!

"Listen, I need to stick around for a bit. Tony called and needs me to work the lunch shift. Are you gonna be ok?"

She genuinely loved him, perhaps more now than ever before.

"I'll be ok," he replied.

Once the world's greatest super hero, Ian Stewart walked out into the cold, late-morning air. By now the city of Everchance was fully awake. All along its crowded streets, people rushed like ants. He was one of them now. Of course, he'd *always* been one of them, but his powers had invariably cut him off.

He knew his abilities were a gift. He also knew his intentions to use them for good was a gift. But somehow, someway, all those gifts had become a curse. Somewhere along the road of being *super* human, he had lost what it meant to be *simply* human. His powers, instead of drawing him closer to those he loved, had kept him isolated in a fortress to keep him in - or maybe to keep others out.

Then a thought hit him. It was so powerful that he came to a dead stop and almost caused a pile-up of people walking too closely on the sidewalk behind him. Maybe his powers were given to him in order to make him more human, not less. Maybe that's why the aliens had reclaimed them. Maybe the alien's greatest gift was not the giving of the powers, but the taking of all of them back to themselves.

As he stood there in the current of people rushing around him, large flakes of every different shape and size began to fall. He had lived the past thirty years of his life amidst a sea of snow. It was always the landscape around the Fortress of Solace. It piled up. It drifted. It covered everything. It never changed. He'd always taken it for granted. Now, as he stood there a free man among equal men, he watched the snow fall as if for the first time. He fixed his eye on one snowflake in particular as it lightly drifted down to rest on his shoulder. He smiled and began to walk again. It was going to be a good day.

Captain Ultra: The Rooftop

For the third time that morning, scalding grease splattered from a pan of frying eggs onto Ian's arm. The kitchen of the Old Times Remembered Diner was sweltering. He had been up since four and at work since five. His skills as a short order cook were steadily improving. When it came to food prep he was outstanding, but the servers insisted he could definitely "step up the pace."

It had been over a year since he had woken to a visit from the aliens who had, within moments, ended his life as Captain Ultra. However, the peace and fulfillment they had wished him hadn't yet arrived. It had taken him three months just to stop having panic attacks over the evening news. In the span of seven months, he had picked up a bottle, got lost in it, and was finally finding his way out. After speaking with Tony, the owner of the diner, Fawn landed Ian a job. She was always graciously covering for him when he had shown up drunk or late for work on more than a few occasions. But Ian felt confident now that the rough spots were slowly getting ironed out. He and Fawn were speaking again, and he was attending an AA meeting at least once a week.

Aside from Fawn, Ian had never revealed his former identity as Captain Ultra to anyone. It took all of his strength to remain quiet when he would overhear what people were saying about him. Some said that Captain Ultra was dead. Wild reports circulated as to just how the hero had met his demise. Others said he had returned to the planet he had come from, galaxies away. And a few, mostly the tabloids, believed he would eventually return after he had finished vacationing in the tropics with his supermodel girlfriend. That was the funniest one of all.

No one would have ever imagined that Captain Ultra was now just an average man. They would never have listened if someone had told them that Captain Ultra was actually the bearded man frying up country ham and bacon behind the counter at the local diner. It was simply not the story that anyone wanted to believe.

Ian's shift ended at two in the afternoon. He couldn't wait to get home and rest his aching feet. Some days he would give anything to have those tireless hero legs again.

As he stepped out the back door of the diner, a boy came running up to him. He hurriedly jammed a crumpled two-dollar bill into Ian's hand and scurried away. Ian knew he looked pretty bad after the breakfast shift but not awful enough to have children offering him money. He straightened out the bill and noticed handwritten words begin to appear where his fingers touched it. He held it in his palm and rubbed it until the complete message was visible:

Meet me tonight on Top of
The McMurray Building
10pm

There was only one person it could have been from…

With suites located on the very top floors, the McMurray building was open all day and night. When Ian arrived, he discovered that the elevators were temporarily out of order.

"Just my luck," he murmured.

The McMurray building was forty-eight stories tall. Forty-eight flights of steps was the most exercise Ian had tackled since he left the Fortress of Solace. By the time he reached the top, he was sweating and gasping for air like an ill-prepared runner trying to complete a marathon. Cautiously he opened the steel door and stepped onto the roof that boasted one of the best views of the city.

The summit of the McMurray building was a wide-open space with only a few large heating and cooling units scattered about. Ian quickly scanned the rooftop but saw no one. Since his host had yet to appear, he strolled over to the edge and peered out at the sprawling metropolis of Everchance. It looked enchanting in the moonlight. A gentle breeze blew free of the stifling air of the city down below making Ian grateful for a moment to fully compose himself before his interview. A brief flash of the past swept through his mind as he took it all in. The last time he stood on this rooftop was after one of his final clashes with Nerofame. Then, from behind him, as if summoned by memory and birthed from shadow, Ian heard the voice of the man himself.

As Ian turned, he hardly recognized the figure before him. All of his memories of Nerofame had him dressed in his red and black body armor. If it hadn't been for the voice, Ian would never have guessed that the man in the pinstripe suit and slicked red hair before him was his former nemesis.

"So it's *true* then," said Nerofame with a note of intrigue in his voice, "You have lost your abilities. Surely Captain Ultra would have never taken forty flights of stairs to reach the top of a building. When you first disappeared, I thought you may be planning to thwart me with some new scheme - but as time went on, I began to suspect something more profound may have occurred after all."

Of all the strange new emotions Ian had felt since his abilities had been reclaimed, fear was one he was still not accustomed to. As he stood before Nerofame, utterly power-less, he felt the alarm begin to rise up within him like never before. Although he had changed profoundly since that fate-ful day a year ago, Nerofame had not. Ian could hear the familiar malice and arrogance dripping from his every word. With caution and a bit of luck, Ian thought he might just sur-vive this encounter. Fortunately, he still remembered how to talk to madmen in a way they understood.

"So what do you want with me now?" said Ian. "I have no abilities. All my superpowers are gone. They're not coming back either. I'm completely defenseless. You've won, Nerofame. I took some battles, but you won the war. What glory is there in killing a man who can't fight back? Isn't it enough to let me live each day suffering over what I've lost?" He hoped something he had said about winning had somehow struck a chord.

When Nerofame had finished laughing he pulled out his handkerchief, dabbed the tears from his eyes, and said, "As pleasurable as it would be to kill you, I would hate to waste such good talent, especially when we have so much in common."

Ian stared back with a puzzled look as Nerofame continued.

"I see that you think you're the only one the aliens gave their extraordinary powers to, but they probably didn't tell you the whole story. You were their *second* choice, Ian. Oh, yes, I know your name...

"Their first choice was a boy, almost ten years older, by the name of Nicholas Fame. He was unwittingly given extraordinary gifts, much like the ones you possessed. But, according to the aliens who reclaimed his powers, he had mis-used them only to secure his own dreams and desires.

"But the boy was no half-wit - oh, no... He was a ge-nius. By the time the aliens had robbed him, he had already devised the means to make up for what they had stolen. He developed a way to fly. He dreamt up new ways to succeed and obtain power. He pulled himself up by his bootstraps and became a god! He became...me.

"So when you came along, I immediately suspect-ed how you must have come by such...skills. It's such a shame you chose to try and stop me. If you had just paused to think for a moment, you would have realized our origins were very much the same. In a strange way, Ian, we're brothers - both teased by these aliens and left with nothing except our wits and courage. But, you don't have to remain powerless, Ian."

Nerofame moved toward a large container, about eight feet in height and covered with a black sheet. He pulled the cover off to reveal a massive glass case. Inside of it, suspended in midair, was a body suit. It shimmered a dark blue as it revolved slowly. It was strikingly similar to the Captain Ultra suit Ian had once worn.

"What you are looking at may be my greatest achievement yet, Ian. This *super*-suit has stretched my genius to new limits. It's bulletproof and hard as steel, yet it weighs almost nothing. It contains lasers in the arms and rockets in the legs for flight, all completely concealed. It can do almost everything you once could do. It is, in itself, Captain Ultra. All it truly needs now is someone with the ability and experience to use it."

Nerofame paused to let his words sink in.

"What are you driving at, Nerofame? What twisted plot are you hatching?" Ian said with the authority of the old Captain Ultra.

"Oh I'm not plotting anything, yet," said Nerofame. "I only come to make an offer: Join me Ian! Make the suit your own and reclaim your powers. Come with me and together we can rule the world. You need only do as I say and soon you will forget all about aliens and their Indian-giving ways. Finally you can erase the nightmare you've lived for the past year as a pathetically normal human."

Ian was dumbstruck. For a split second he thought about just how wonderful it would be to have his old life back again. But the asking price was too high. He would rather be free and powerless than seated on top of the world, chained like a prisoner. He knew if he turned down Nerofame's proposal, it would never be offered again. But no matter who wore the suit, it would only be as Nerofame's puppet and used for his bidding.

Ian stood lost in thought for a moment and then replied, "You paint quite the picture, Nerofame… quite the picture indeed. You make domination, power, and elitism seem like the most natural things in the world - as if the noblest idea ever conceived is to be separated from everyone else. But that's just not how it works. I'm tired of living like there are two different worlds: mine and everyone else's. There's only one world, and it works best when we realize that we're all connected in it. Sorry to disappoint you, but I'd rather live in that world."

Ian turned and began to head for the door that led to the stairs. He braced himself for what might be coming. Nerofame could eliminate him in a heartbeat. He suspected that while his back was turned, Nerofame was probably reaching for his Thermo-gun. He had almost reached the door and placed his hand on the latch when Nerofame's voice drew him back in.

"I always suspected Captain Ultra was big on muscle and short on brains. You truly are a fool, Ian. If you won't serve by my side, you will bow to me within a few months after I take over the world. Power is what makes the world go around, and I will soon have all of it. And if you try to stop me I will kill you, Ian. I'll kill you, that is, after I make you watch me dispose of your Fawn first."

Ian paused for an instant and felt the rage rise up within him. He couldn't let it get the best of him now if he wanted to somehow, one day, stop Nerofame. Without a word he pulled the handle on the door to the stairs.

It was a long walk back down the forty-eight floors. By the time he reached the halfway point, he had paused at least a dozen times to catch his breath and his thoughts.

There were moments everything inside of him wanted to run back up and accept Nerofame's offer. Then there were other times he couldn't run down fast enough to find Fawn, take her in his arms, and never let her go again.

When he reached the bottom he looked at his cell phone and realized that he should have been in bed three hours ago. He had to be at work in the morning.

Exiting the building, the city throbbed with a life that Ian hadn't noticed in the quiet stillness on the top of the McMurray building. Everchance was teeming with energy. The taxicabs plowed through the steam pouring from the street grates. Cars and buses honked their horns and maneuvered through the changing traffic lights. Clubs, restaurants, and theaters drew lines of people. Couples strolled, hands entangled, having intimate conversations. Vagabonds sat in alleys or begged for change. Thousands of people moved in every direction as Ian Stewart made his way back to his small apartment on the east side, happily, among it all.

Hogard
A Fairy Tale

This is a story concerning a very persistent giant and a far superior elf…

Hogard the Giant, also known as Hogard the Terrible, and in some places, Hogard the Destroyer, was the last of his kind. All of the other giants had either died off or been killed in battles by the race of men.

Tragically, Hogard's last remaining brother, Hobweed the Hunter, was also killed at the hands of men. Infuriated by his death, Hogard swore revenge. He solemnly vowed that he would make war upon and completely destroy the city of Belcloud that harbored his brother's murderers.

With his great club ready to smash and his face screwed up in a look to cause utmost terror, Hogard arrived at the city gates only to discover an unwelcome crinkle in his plan. What he did not foresee was that a certain elf, by the name of Jedric Trugrace, was guarding the gate protecting the city of Belcloud.

"Welcome Hogard, beloved giant. I was wondering when you would arrive to take your revenge," said the elf.

"Stand aside, elf," said Hogard, "I have business here that does not concern you. I mean to smash and destroy every last living thing in yonder city."

"I'm afraid I cannot let you do that dear ol' friend," said the elf. "You see, the King of Belcloud has hired me to protect this fair domain from any attack you may attempt. I'm sorry, but I'm afraid your anger will have to be vented elsewhere."

On hearing this, Hogard flew into a fierce tantrum. He threw himself about, huffing and fuming in complete frustration until his face was red and there were great drops of sweat running down his arms.

Now you may think that Hogard, being a giant, would have had every physical advantage over the elf so that he could simply step on him like a bug or club him like a piñata and be about his business. But this is where you have believed mere fantasies! For since the days of his childhood, Hogard had heard the amazing stories of the powerful magic, great cunning, and impeccable wisdom possessed by elves. The giant knew only too well that it would be impossible to win the day. Thus rebuffed, Hogard slunk back to his home among the mountain passes.

Of course it is common knowledge that what giants may lack in brains they easily make up for in persistence. Alas, after many sleepless nights, Hogard came up with a clever plan to deceive Jedric and, thereby, enter the city of Belcloud.

It was mid-morning of the following day. The elf was faithfully at his station once more when he spied Hogard strolling toward the main gate...dressed as a woman.

Hogard, in his best womanly voice croaked, "Oh mighty elven prince, I ask your favor to allow me entrance into your fair city."

"Dear lady," replied Jedric, "if you wanted to fool someone into thinking you're a woman, you really should have shaved your beard and selected a more flattering dress. Pink fabric with orange flowers is completely repulsive, does nothing for your complexion, and clashes with your deerskin handbag... You're not getting in. I know it's you, Hogard."

"How do you know?!" said Hogard, forgetting to disguise his voice. "I mean, ah... how do you know?" returning again to his high-pitched strain.

"Hogard, I would know those bulging arms and devilishly furry legs anywhere!" the elf replied, rolling his eyes.

Rejected once more, Hogard the Terrible made his way back home. He trudged away, ripping off the dress so that his reputation would not be further damaged by such out-of-style fashions.

Now a mighty river ran from the mountain range where Hogard made his dwelling, all the way to the city of Belcloud. It rolled down the plain until it flowed directly behind the great city. Once again, Hogard devised what he thought to be a brilliantly sneaky plan. As quietly as a giant possibly could, he would swim down the river to Belcloud until he came up behind the unsuspecting city. From there, outflanking both Jedric and the city's defenses, Hogard would emerge from the river and sack the place before the elf even knew he was there.

Everything went as the giant had planned until he

emerged from the river behind Belcloud. As he pulled himself up onto the riverbank, there stood Jedric the Elf.

"Good day, mighty Hogard. Out for a morning swim?"

Hogard knew that he had been foiled once again and that his watery, backdoor siege was completely ruined.

"You can't guard this city forever Jedric!" said the giant angrily. "One day you're bound to grow tired and make a mistake, so you might as well let me pass now."

But the elf replied, "Return a million times and a million times you will find me here. You cannot go around me, trick me, or subdue me. You must, therefore, go through me. Go home, Hogard."

"Home I'll go," said Hogard, "but I'll return, for we giants never give up."

"And I will be waiting," said the elf.

The giant, true to his word, did not give up. As sure as the sunrise, once a week for the next year, Hogard came again and again to the city gates of Belcloud. Sometimes he would try to disguise himself or sneak past Jedric with groups of travelers, but Hogard was much too large to blend into a crowd. Other times he would try to offer the elf bribes with great sacks of gold. Once, he even borrowed a wizard's wand to try to cast a spell upon Jedric, but it backfired and turned poor Hogard into a monstrous chicken for a time. No matter how he tried, the giant was thwarted each and every time. He could not trick or strike a deal with the savvy elf.

Then one day after a full year of being denied entrance into the city of Belcloud, Hogard sat in a nearby forest looking upon the hated place, drinking ale, and feeling terribly sorry for himself. And as he sat there, glaring at his enemies, his rage began to simmer and boil until something inside of Hogard finally snapped. Furiously he threw the ale aside, picked up his mighty club, and began to run straight for the city. If he could not go around the elf, he would go through him.

Hogard charged the city gates at full speed with his club waving wildly over his head. From behind the gates, the people of Belcloud felt the earth shake. They screamed in fear as they saw the giant's reckless approach. It was a sight that would have alarmed anyone - anyone except Jedric, of course. The elf defending the gate quietly stood his ground.

The giant was close now, within moments he would be upon the elf and the cowering city. Just as Hogard began to raise his enormous club, light shot out of the elf's staff as he pointed it at the oncoming monster, bringing him to a screeching halt. It bathed him in its glow. Then, Jedric began to sing. It was a quiet but hauntingly beautiful melody. It was the ancient song.

At first, the giant seemed confused and even more enraged. It looked as if he desperately wanted to charge ahead but couldn't - as if he were being held fast by arms even larger than his own. And as he heard the ancient song and felt the warmth rush through him, something remarkable happened inside of Hogard: his heart broke. Well, not his *heart* actually. It was more like the crust around the giant's heart began to crumble away. All the hatred and malice that Hogard had collected over the years began to shudder and break apart, leaving the giant weeping upon his knees.

Jedric's song slowly died away and the glow of the light from his staff diminished. All was quiet as the people breathlessly watched from their windows and wondered what would happen next.

When the giant finally looked up, the people gasped. His face had been changed. Oh, it was still the same Hogard with his wild hair and wooly beard, but now he looked rested and peaceful, and somehow younger than ever before. All of the scars that had once marred his limbs and face from the many years of countless battles had all but disappeared. The elf and his ancient song had utterly changed the heart of the giant.

Instantly, the giant's threat to the good people of Belcloud was no more. In time, Hogard "the Terrible" became Hogard "the True." And Hogard "the Destroyer" became known as Hogard "the Friend." In fact, he came to be a welcomed guest, like that of a favorite uncle coming to town for a visit. The children of Belcloud giggled with glee when he would sound his ferocious laugh. And they would dance with joy at his feet, for they knew that in his huge pockets were toys and treats for them all. Their parents would sigh with great relief knowing that Hogard, now a trusted ally rather than a fearsome enemy, would defend them all to the death if ever their great city were in peril.

Hogard the Giant and Jedric the Elf became fast friends and their adventures together are now tales of fantastic legend. They were as close as two friends could be, often sitting up late at night smoking their pipes while discussing the mysteries of their strange world. Oddly, the incident that had brought them together that fateful day was never brought up between them. And whenever others would mention the occasion to them, Hogard would chuckle and change the subject, while the elf would act like he simply didn't remember.

Sparrow,

As you're digesting these odd tales I thought I might include a scene I happened to witness on a number of occasions.

Some months after his encounter with Merrit, F.T. began to spend more and more of his time at the tavern and less and less at the parish. His fellow friars considered his "work" strictly an outreach to the lost and so they questioned little without suspicions being raised.

However, something quite different was occurring. He was looking at the world through brand new eyes. Where once he saw himself as the sole light-bearer, he now saw light from every corner of the room and in every person. Where once he believed only the penitent sinner and remorseful wretch could earn God's favor, he now began to live in the assurance that no human attitude or action could change the stubborn heart of the Father. God loved and accepted, period.

What a fool he had been! His Savior's Spirit was in them all. He heard his Master's voice in their songs and stories. On any given night you could hear him trade jokes over a pint with the town drunk. You could catch him at a corner table sharing his tales of the scandalous love of God.

With a wry smile, a twinkle in his eye, and an ever-rounding belly he became a lover, not only of the finest ale but of all people. It was with my own eyes I saw him often place his hand on the back of many a downcast person, and firmly proclaim, "You too have been included in the Great Embrace... Awaken and enjoy!"

All the same, there were those in the crowd who did not care for such pronouncements: religious spirits and spies. To witness this man of the cloth loudly announcing God's affirming nod without any prescribed religious duties was blasphemy. To see him eat and drink with them, like they were all of the same standing in the divine light was shocking and, to say the least, completely forbidden. If such ideas had time to grow in the hearts of men, religion and its towers made of matchsticks would be toppled. Such heresies could not be allowed to continue.

Which reminds us, dear Sparrow, as long as man seeks to appease what he perceives to be an angry God and his towers of Babel stand, the message of love and unconditional acceptance is endangered. Share these stories wisely. Truth is never completely out of the woods.

Limner

The Circus

The circus had just ended as laughing children and smiling parents burst through the doors of the downtown arena. They had spent the last two hours happily lost in a world of sheer wonder, complete with elephants, clowns, tigers, and acrobats. The kids were still oozing with energy as they darted around the grown-ups like banshees, clanging and banging the noisemakers their parents had bought them…but now it was time to go home.

The mass exodus commenced as the crowds made their way back to their cars parked up and down the city streets or in the parking garages nearby. The crossing guards and police herded them. It had been raining, making the late November afternoon rather dreary, damp, and cold.

They had set up on a corner about two blocks from the arena, near a large parking garage. Some of the group, about ten people, stood handing out what looked to be little pamphlets to the passersby. Other members of the small band had made themselves into human billboards, wearing signs and placards that said things like, "Turn or Burn!", "Repent or Perish!", "God will Judge the Sexually Immoral," and "He Who Sins Shall Surely Die!"

As people made their way around the billboards, a member of the group was shouting at the crowd through a bullhorn. He looked to be in his mid-forties with a slight stomach, mustache, and baseball cap that announced "Jesus Saves" on it. Without the bullhorn, he could easily have passed for a plumber, but today he was something entirely different. Today he was a messenger spreading the good news. The bullhorn was turned up as loud as it could go, and he was shouting so fiercely that it was hard to distinguish exactly what he was saying. At times, however, words like "eternal fire" and "repent" made his otherwise garbled point. He certainly looked angry - he was red in the face and working up a sweat as he boldly stood and proclaimed his message.

Most of the crowd coming from the arena walked past the small band of true believers without so much as a glance. Some just rolled their eyes and walked on. Others gave a gruff "no thank you" and hurried along. Some parents picked up their kids and hurried through the pack of evangelists like they were trying to save their children from a burning building.

A few unwittingly took a pamphlet only to look at it, realize what it contained, and angrily stuff it in their pockets. Still, others couldn't avoid making eye contact that led to questions like, "Are you saved?" or "Do you know where you'll go when you die?" One young man had been cornered near a trashcan by two members of the group for showing a trace of interest in their message. The look on his face now assured others they didn't want to make the same mistake.

Although they were odd and seemingly out of place,

the faithful pack of evangelists was not to be trifled with. They made it abundantly clear that anyone who expressed disagreement with them would burn in hell, and that for all eternity.

She had taken up a spot on the opposite corner, unnoticed, when the main bulk of circus attendees met with the band across the street. The young girl wore torn blue jeans and a grey t-shirt. She had straight dark hair pulled back in a ponytail from which a number of shiny strands had already escaped. Staring toward the opposite corner, she sat silently with a smile on her face. In her hands she held a sign written on white tagboard with one word scrawled upon it:

Love

It only took a few minutes before she began to draw attention. Those who had already been verbally accosted began to cheer for her and applaud. Some gave her thumbs up as they walked away from their unsuccessful discussions. Cars passing by honked their horns in appreciation of her message. Some were even inspired to laugh at and heckle the group on the opposite corner now that someone had finally given a non-verbal voice to what their hearts felt. She sat still like a soldier - her only weapon a one-word sign.

The members of the group tried to ignore the girl. Escalating their efforts, they attempted to divert the people's attention away from her. They shouted louder and waved their Bibles like swords, but it soon became apparent that she was silently winning the day.

The group, however, had not come all the way into the city to be upstaged or have their message contradicted in any way. Soon, some of them began to point and scream at her from across the street. They told her to go away, but she would not. They shouted at the passersby to ignore her, "lest their souls perish."

Finally, the man with the bullhorn began to address the girl seated on the neighboring corner. Yet again, most of his words were lost in volume and venom - although pronouncements of "devil," "whore," and "hell" came through loud and clear.

The girl sat calmly, staring at him.

With each word, he grew louder and more hateful as his anger continued to escalate.

Seeing that he was getting nowhere, he must have thought she was not hearing him clearly - that a closer proximity would help him succeed in removing the distraction. The man crossed the street against the traffic light, walked up to the girl, and began to yell at her. The only difference between his message from afar and this one was the absence of the bullhorn that he now held at his side. Still, the young girl sat quietly, looking straight ahead facing the opposite side of the street. She paid no attention to the older man standing above her screaming in her ear.

Those who happened to be standing on the corner waiting to cross the street started to take notice. A few of the male pedestrians began to turn their attention to the man.

"Hey buddy, back off!"

"Leave her alone, pal."

Ignoring their pleas, the man with the bullhorn

continued his tirade. Meanwhile, another member of the group had crossed the street and joined the man. He tugged on his arm in an attempt to pull him away.

"Come on Jack, leave her alone. We've got to get back to the van."

The other members of the group had forgotten their duties by now and stood on the opposite corner curiously watching the scene unfold.

But the man would not be distracted. He violently jerked his arm away from his friend and, in doing so, slashed the girl across the face with his bullhorn. She slumped over to her side with her hands to her face, a torrent of blood pouring from her mouth and nose.

The man stood there wide-eyed and shocked at what he had done. Gasps and screams erupted around him as another man's fist landed squarely on his jaw, almost knocking him into the street. Another spectator grabbed the other evangelist and began to wrestle him to the ground. More members of the group came streaming across the intersection to stop or join the fight. Soon, at least a dozen people were engrossed in the mêlée.

Police came from every direction. The members of the group that had occupied the opposite corner fled - the man with the bullhorn being the first to run when the sirens started. But the scene was mostly abandoned by the time the authorities arrived. Only a few witnesses remained to give an account of what they had seen.

After the police had finished gathering information, the girl with the sign was nowhere to be found. Somehow she had managed to disappear amidst the struggle on the street corner, now quiet again. All that remained was a blood-stained sign covered with dirt and footprints, lying in the gutter.

The Last Sermon

The funeral was set to begin at eleven sharp, but people just kept pouring into the old church sanctuary. Soon enough, folding chairs were placed in the aisle. By twenty after, it was standing room only. The small house of worship was filled with the smell of cheap roses, embalming fluid, and warm bodies in the mid-April heat.

They had all come with full hearts for the deceased. Reverend Billings had ministered at Saint Stevens Baptist Church for over thirty years. He also had built a fine reputation abroad, serving on various mission boards and speaking at numerous conventions. His sacrifice and service were widely known.

Now gone to his eternal rest, many came to pay their final respects to the good reverend. In their hearts, everyone carried fond memories of the way Reverend Billings had touched their lives. Each person had a story to share. He had been there for them in their sickness and health. As they solemnly waited for the service to begin they quietly reminisced about his kind words, gentle manner, stirring sermons, and most importantly, his godly air.

Surely, Saint Stevens would have never survived without Reverend Billings. It was his guidance and preaching that kept the once failing church alive. It was his encouragement that guided them to further their potential, and his vision that allowed their fellowship to grow larger. In the difficult times of layoffs, failed marriages, and death, he inspired them when all hope had dimmed. A grateful throng now poured into the church to say, "thank you" as best they could.

The performing of the service and eulogy had fallen to Reverend Daniels, the associate minister to Reverend Billings. He was a young man in his early thirties with a slender body, an awkward smile, and a willing spirit. Unfortunately, he was rarely taken seriously in many of his duties. Most of the congregation saw him as a poor replacement to the great Reverend Billings. When Daniels first arrived, he could see the resentment in their faces. They were all thinking the same thing: that in due season, Daniels would assume Reverend Billings' duties and undoubtedly fail to live up to him. Watching Reverend Daniels receive mourners, however, smiling kindly upon all who passed by the casket, gave many a sense of stability. It was a mild comfort knowing that Reverend Billings had chosen Reverend Daniels to follow him in shepherding his beloved congregation. Certainly Reverend Billings had chosen wisely, leaving the flock to assume they were still in good hands.

With a slow mournful moan, the organ began to play. People pressed tightly into the hard wooden pews. Many began to fan themselves with a small handbill that had been given to them as they came in.

After the singing of the first hymn, Reverend Daniels rose to speak. As he slowly made his way to the pulpit, he could already tell by the fervency and passion of the singing that expectations were high today. He could feel the weight of the moment. Much was riding upon it. People were aching to have their hearts comforted and to see just due given to this man who had meant so very much to them all.

Reverend Daniels launched into a rather typical opening greeting, followed by a reading of the Twenty-Third Psalm. He then proceeded to outline Reverend Billings' life in broad strokes. Reverend Billings' accomplishments were stunning. Sympathetic "amens," agreements, and sobs could be heard as Reverend Billings' history was laid out in black and white. All in all, Reverend Daniels had done well. He had carefully collected all the family stories and pertinent facts. He had interviewed many close friends and associates for the more obscure, but heartwarming views into Billings' life as well. However, he knew that the closing of the service would be magical, ultimately leaving the congregation riveted and uplifted.

"As you all well know, Reverend Billings was a gifted preacher and communicator of the gospel. A few weeks ago, before his passing, I met with him. It was at that time that Reverend Billings gave me a video of what he called 'my last sermon.' He expressed to me that it was not to be played until his memorial service. He told me that he wanted it to be a gift to you, knowing you would need comfort in this difficult time. So without further ado, to close out his own memorial service, I give you Reverend David Billings..."

The lights in the church dimmed. Behind the pulpit,

on the screen above the stage, appeared an elderly man in a hospital gown, sitting in a green vinyl chair. His white hair was tousled, his face gaunt, and his body, frail and feeble. An IV stood beside the chair with a line running into the old man's bruised arm. His eyes were peaceful and his familiar smile conveyed that sense of calm urgency he had always preached with. As he appeared, a collective sigh of adoration went up from the congregation.

Greetings, friends and family. Welcome to my memorial service. As a preacher, one is regularly given a chance to say many things. Week after week, it is a privilege to convey the deep truths of God, speak the encouraging words of a shepherd, or utter the stern admonishments of a father. Yet, after all these years of preaching, I still feel that I have not said nearly enough of what I could have, or should have, shared with you. With that being said, I now wish to deliver to you my final sermon, if you will...

Reverend Billings paused briefly for dramatic effect.

Now, I have never advocated confession to any man, nor assumed a spoken confession to be necessary, but it is important to me that you know what kind of man to which you say goodbye to today. It's important you see the things I want to share with you and that you see them about yourselves as well.

A stuffy heat had crept into the old building and people began to shift in their seats. Of course, it may have been that they were just settling in, realizing that Reverend Billings was going to speak for a few more minutes. But possibly, it was that they sensed something unwelcome coming on - the way animals sense bad weather approaching or the tickling feeling one gets in the throat before coming down with the flu.

For starters, let me just say that ministry was more of a curse than a blessing. I know I began for good reasons... but why I continued for so long, I haven't quite been able to figure out. The constant pressure and criticism was enough to drive a man to the brink of madness! The saints of old spoke of what they called "the dark night of the soul." Well, you'd better believe I've seen it. I've had my share of late nights, wondering if I should just end my time on earth quickly rather than endure! Oh, I know I put up a good front, but honestly, if it weren't for the bottle and an occasional puff of marijuana, I probably would have killed myself years ago...

The gentle smile on Reverend Daniels' face began to melt. He started to shift around, possibly searching for the nearest exit. The organist glared at him, as if he somehow knew this was coming. However, as their eyes met, it became mutually obvious that he did not and that they were now the unfortunate witnesses of a train wreck in slow motion.

Most in the congregation sat with their mouths agape. Most, that is, except what was left of Reverend Billings' remaining relatives. If the ghost of Billings himself had casually strolled into the room, they would not have been more shocked. Murmurs and small wailing sounds began to issue from the front rows. Second by second, the situation was growing more and more surreal. Mothers began to put their hands over their children's ears as Reverend Billings had now launched into a string of profanity, bemoaning the perils of his earthly calling.

Every man is given to lust... I am a man. Often I was given to lust and had numerous affairs. The names and the dates are inconsequential now...

At this point, a careful observer would have noticed at least three different women in the congregation studying their program with all earnestness and two former church secretaries quietly slip out.

I have, at times, stolen money from this very church. The amounts and times vary in degrees, but I always found a way to repay the amounts and cover my tracks...

Looking back, Reverend Daniels, who is currently no longer in ministry, wished he had the presence of mind to have the accursed video turned off or sprint back to the soundboard and put an end to it himself. Alas, Reverend Daniels, although well meaning, was never very fast on his feet. Hopelessly paralyzed by shock, he could not make it stop, despite a few pleading voices from the congregation for him to do just that.

But none of these sins of the flesh compare to the worst of my crimes: my sins of pride, jealousy, and utter hypocrisy. I grew this church based on my lack of self worth and kept it full by preaching sermons I half-believed. I was a poor husband and a bad father...

The old man broke down. His frail body vibrated with unheard sobs as silence momentarily filled the room. But as he composed himself, looking once more at the camera, a faint smile crossed his face. It was a sly, scandalous smile - one of knowing something that nobody else knew.

I am now home and at rest in my Father's arms. I cannot change the past by these confessions, but only hope they serve you well in the truth they reveal. Regardless of how you feel about all I've said and done, I am now safe from your judgment and wrath, just as you are safe from mine...as well as my shortcomings and failures. Through all my wanderings and fakery, through all my good days and bad days, I now see that I was never unloved or forsaken. I have always been and always will be His child. I now make my dwelling in The Light's embrace despite what you may think or feel at the moment ... So long, dear friends, until we meet again...

The video winked out as the screen went dark once more. Sobs and angry bursts of disbelief and outrage could be heard throughout the sanctuary. A small riot looked as though it might ensue. Reverend Daniels thought he might have a chance to save it if only he could find the right words. But as he rose to officially conclude the service, his legs seemed to have turned to stone. By the time he made his way back to the pulpit, most of the mourners had begun to file out through the exits.

The few who could still bear to listen, or left seated, heard Reverend Daniels painfully stammer out a handful of random verses.

"Let he who is without sin cast the fi...first stone... Judge not lest ye be judged!"

It was obviously not the conclusion he had planned on, and his impromptu sermonizing was suspect at best.

As most of the mourners headed for the door, almost no one looked back at him. The people had heard enough. In shock and utter disbelief, they left looking down at their feet or plaintively at one another through misty eyes. They felt betrayed, uncaringly blindsided by the old preacher's confession. Here they had come, convinced they were burying a saint, only to find they were burying a sinner.

Treadwalla

The town of Treadwalla was a dot on a map. No one famous anyone had ever heard of had come from there. Like most small towns, it had a main street with a few quaint places to eat lunch and a general store to buy a new shoestring if yours broke. It came complete with a red brick school and a flower shop with a pink door, a disorganized post office, and an official-looking courthouse. It also contained its share of secrets and mysteries that most, who were privy to these oddities, never spoke of. Some, under the promise of anonymity, say that the town was cursed, spawning all sorts of strange people with bizarre gifts. Others say that Treadwalla was, in fact, located upon a "thin place," where the supernatural intermingled with the earthly on a daily basis. Regardless of these curious persons, however, most people living in Treadwalla never spoke of them for fear of being seen as peculiar by the outside world. What was stranger still was that even though Treadwalla was absolutely teeming with abnormality, the town especially shunned those who could not easily hide their own special brand of it. Emeeca was one of those...

Emeeca was orphaned soon after birth when it became obvious to her parents that she cast no shadow by day or night. You could stand her in the middle of an open field on a clear afternoon and no shadow would fall. Obviously this gift made her unique and the object of much torment and ridicule from the other children. It certainly didn't help that atop Emeeca's head she sprouted jet-black hair with a bluish hue, but she never let the scorn of others get to her. Just as light never made her a source of shade, so the constant teasing never brought a frown to her freckled face nor stole her positive outlook on life. Truth be told, it was her cheerfulness and inquisitive nature that helped her get along with almost anyone. It was also how the trouble began.

Emeeca was eleven years old when she, after eleven whole years of never asking for anything like an explanation, asked an innocent question about a taboo subject in Mr. Bumbigulow's history class.

"Mr. B, why is it that everyone in Treadwalla is so strange?"

Mr. B., completely unprepared for such a random and inappropriate question, adjusted his shirt collar and did his level best to downplay the topic.

"My dear young lady, whatever are you talking about?"

Emeeca explained further, "Everyone in Treadwalla seems to have weird things about them, but no one talks about it. Mr. Garbo's dog, Sam, is older than me and has somehow survived his whole life on bologna and beer. And I know for a fact that Mr. Kent has a tree growing in his backyard that blooms starfish and red high-topped sneakers every time it snows. Or what about Mrs. Hodges? She wears a veil over her face everywhere she goes. Then there's

Deanna Smirks...she raises the most beautiful flowers that only bloom in the moonlight!"

Mr. B was shocked by the girl's knowledge.

"Young lady, you obviously have a highly developed imagination and an immense capacity for story-telling, but in this class we deal with facts, not fiction. Now, as I was saying..."

However, Emeeca was not satisfied with this answer, for it was not really an answer at all. She knew these things to be true and had seen them with her very own eyes. Although the people she had mentioned did their best to hide their quirks, Emeeca was not fooled by them. She rarely spied on anyone. No, most of her knowledge came from being curious, polite, and remarkably intelligent for her age. So she went and said something that got her into trouble. She interrupted Mr. B.'s attempt to salvage his lecture with, "Mr. B., is it true that Treadwalla is cursed? Or is it like what Mr. Stimplestein says, that angels use Treadwalla as a holding area for wayward spirits? Or is it like my friend Portico says, that Treadwalla may actually be an alien..."

"That is quite enough you little freak!" Mr. B shouted having finally lost his temper. "You will not hijack my class-room with your childish fantasies. Away with you! Leave this classroom at once, and I suggest that when you return tomorrow you concern yourself with history and not super-stitious nonsense!"

With that, Emeeca was tossed out of school for be-ing observant, asking too many questions, and challenging popular ignorance.

It was still the early afternoon when Emeeca found

herself with nothing to do, so she decided to visit some friends around town. She didn't get along very well with the other children since most of them were frightened of her. Most of Emeeca's friends were adults.

First she went by Ms. Raphael's place. Ms. Raphael was a round little woman with unruly red hair who always wore funny hats with plastic fruit glued to them. She was exceptionally kind and always offered Emeeca her pick of knick-knacks lying around the house whenever she came to visit. The farmhouse was certainly old with no electricity. Ms. Raphael kept hundreds of candles in each and every room to illuminate the place at night. She said she preferred to live the "old-fashioned way." Oddly, every time Ms. Raphael would go shopping in town, the lights in the stores would mysteriously flicker and die out as soon as she stepped inside. But, unfortunately, Ms. Raphael was not at home.

Emeeca then decided to pay a visit to her friend Portico who lived on the outskirts of town. On her way though, she came to a large white church seated at the corner of Elm and Polyphonic. She had never been in a church before, nor given much thought to what went on inside of one. Being naturally inquisitive she decided she would go in and have a look around. Carefully opening the heavy oak door, Emeeca saw that the plain building was only a crude wrapper for an ornate sanctuary. A maroon carpet led down the center aisle to a platform in the front. Fixtures sparkled in gold. There were many people already seated inside. She recognized some faces, but most she did not. All of them were intently listening to someone speaking at the front.

Immediately, Emeeca knew the man dressed all in black as Reverend Jonah.

Reverend Jonah had a reputation around town for being a sober-minded individual who dismissed common enjoyments to keep his mind on holier things. Because of his pious nature, most of the children of Treadwalla, and even some adults, were afraid of him. He was also one of the oldest living people in Treadwalla, well into his nineties.

Emeeca quickly darted into the dimly lit room and had a seat in the last row by the door to listen.

Reverend Jonah spoke in a stage whisper, but he made his voice rise in volume and inflection when he uttered certain words. Emeeca had never heard anyone speak like this before. She was instantly drawn into what the old man had to say.

"Brothers and sisters, we all know we live in terrible times. Our world is full of evil. This town is saturated with it! Abomination stands on the corner. We all know of whom I speak... I speak of those who are full of mischief, the devil's seed, and walk among us, polluting all that is good. They are accursed! For in their bodies and circumstances, they cannot hide the fact that they are the very dwelling of wretchedness."

Emeeca was surprised to see so many people nodding their heads in agreement.

Reverend Jonah threw his arms open wide and clenched his fists for added effect.

"But you and I are different! We are the chosen, and the Light has made a distinction between us and them! We must purge the evil from among us and among this town!"

Emeeca's heart was pounding. Was Reverend Jonah referring to all the strange people that filled Treadwalla? Was he talking about her friends and the people she loved most? Was he talking about her?

Just then, as Emeeca sat lost in thought, Reverend Jonah paused. His piercing gaze quickly scanned the room and then came to rest on her. He pointed his finger and began to yell from the front.

"You there…seated in the back! You are one of them, aren't you? You are one who comes seeking the truth because you cannot hide your wickedness!"

Emeeca looked over her shoulder, hoping he was speaking to someone else, but she was the last row. Reverend Jonah began to slowly amble down the aisle in her direction, his bloodshot eyes glistening in the soft light.

"You are but an orphan, an urchin child, wandering away from school and all that is good," Jonah said.

Everyone in the room was now turned and looking at her.

"You must come into the light, child," he continued. "But first, you must be free from the demons that have cursed you and this fair town for too long! Be healed and be free!"

Before she could react, Reverend Jonah was beside her. He grabbed her shoulder with one hand and pushed her down to her knees. He placed his other hand on her head and began to yell in her ear.

"Demon, come out! Evil spirit that dwells within this child and causes her to cast no shadow, be gone!"

In her wildest dreams, Emeeca never thought a curious visit would end up this way. She knelt, trembling under the weight of the preacher's grasp. With every other word, Emeeca felt the hand on her head push down for added emphasis. For over ten minutes Reverend Jonah carried on and screamed at whatever he thought may be living inside of her, commanding it to leave. Obviously, Reverend Jonah was expecting something to happen. Emeeca, however, couldn't possibly imagine something more dramatic taking place.

After what seemed like an eternity of waiting for Reverend Jonah to conclude his exorcism, Emeeca was surprised that the old man still had more to give. He launched into stamping his feet and chanting in some kind of language Emeeca had never heard. She couldn't help but laugh.

Stopping, mid-chant, Reverend Jonah took his hands off the girl.

"You mock the Light's servant, child?"

Emeeca quieted her giggle for a moment and looked up at him with a smile.

"Reverend Jonah! I didn't know you had strange abilities too! You sound like Mrs. Bangarang when she gets those fits every time it rains and starts dancing and singing in the street! Of course," Emeeca added, "she only tries to do it now in her backyard since people started making comments…"

She never saw the back of Reverend Jonah's hand coming, nor thought it would sting as much as it did, until she had landed like a ragdoll on the carpet. Her cheek burned like fire as warm tears began to fill her eyes and spill out. No one in the congregation looked surprised that he had struck the child. Rather, they seemed in complete agreement with his actions toward the girl looking up from the floor.

"Spawn of demons! Leave this house of truth and never return! Go back to live with those possessed malformations you come from! This is a place for those whose souls have been swept clean, not for dirty little children who cast no shadow!"

Jonah pointed his bony finger at the door.

Emeeca scrambled to her feet and bolted out of the entrance to the dark sanctuary into the bright light of the sun. As she stood on the corner in bewilderment, sobs began to break in waves from deep inside making her chest heave. Her cheek still burned and her head was beginning to throb like a bell after it had been rung too forcefully. Relieved to be free of Reverend Jonah, but still in complete shock, she remembered where she had been going. She raced for Portico's house.

Emmet Portico lived on the very edge of Treadwalla in a small shack that was hidden by trees. He never ventured into town and had most of his necessities delivered to him. Just like Emeeca, Portico's differences were not easily hidden. The people of Treadwalla feared him and spoke occasionally of "that freak" that lived out in the woods. Parents would never let their children play near his home in the forest for fear that "old clown-face" might snatch them.

When Emmet was twelve years old, a circus passed through Treadwalla. He had never been to a circus, but he longed to see the exotic animals and daring performers in sequined tights, walking on high wires. His parents strictly forbade it though. They told him it was not a place for cultured people. On the final night of the circus, however, against his parent's orders, Emmet snuck out of his house to go and see the big tent rising out of a nearby meadow.

The show was over by the time he arrived, but instead of going back home, Emmet decided to take a stroll through all of the cages and wagons being prepared to leave the next day. He was completely ignored with all of the hustle and bustle going on. Animals were being fed and tents were being folded by rough-looking circus hands. He paused by the tigers in their cages and wished he had been able to see them stand on their hind legs like the pictures he had seen in magazines. He also goggled at all the marvelous circus characters like the strong man and the bearded lady wandering past him absorbed in conversation. Although, what Emmet loved most were the clowns. He happened to see a few walk by, still dressed in their funny costumes, joking and laughing with one another. He followed them.

As he trailed the clowns, one dressed in an orange suit noticed him. He told Emmet that the show was over and that he had to go home. The boy replied that he had missed the show and was just having a look around. The clown, whose stage name was Ritiglio, took pity on him for missing the show. He liked the boy's sense of adventure and invited him into the clown's trailer to have a look around. Emmet jumped at the chance.

Once inside, he couldn't believe his eyes. He was actually standing in the place where the clowns lived and prepared. The performers seemed to enjoy having the boy visit. Some of them showed him tricks like pulling flowers out of their funny hats or smashing their fingers with rubber hammers.

But the highlight of the visit was when Ritiglio offered to paint Emmet's face like a clown! He watched in the mirror as Ritiglio applied the white base and then the black and brown makeup around his lips and eyes. The lines were crisp and beautifully done. Ritiglio had given Emmet a sad clown face. He thought it appropriate since Emmet didn't get to see the show.

His visit with the clowns ended too soon. He thanked Ritiglio and his friends, hurrying home to wash the makeup off of his face and crawl back into bed before his parents discovered his absence.

But when he tried to wash his face, the makeup Ritiglio had applied would not come off. No matter how much soap and water he used or how hard he scrubbed, the clown face would not disappear. The sad mask was permanently attached.

What followed was tragic. Emmet's parents, along with the rest of Treadwalla, disowned him. No school or orphanage would have him. By the time it occurred to him to run away and join up with the circus, they were already gone. Nothing was left for Emmet but to become the most infamous outcast of Treadwalla - a calling he, in time, lived up to.

He educated himself and, with little help, learned to survive in the wild alone. Yet, for all he had been through, he still remained friendly, but rather aloof. His bizarre appearance and strange ways left most people uncomfortable, so they stayed clear of his dwelling in the woods. The few friends he did have rarely came by, but when they did, they called him by his last name, Portico.

Soon Emeeca arrived at the shack in the woods. It was built in the shape of an octagon out of scrap wood, tree branches, and mud. The front door was triangular and there were odd colored sheets hanging in the windows. Inside on the walls hung framed photos of various people. Emeeca never knew, or asked, who they were though because all of the faces had been torn out of the pictures.

She had stopped crying by now, but her face was still blotched and streaked from tears.

She found Portico standing outside, talking to Captain Riggins, whom everyone called Captain Rigs. Captain Rigs was a fisherman that never caught a single fish. He had a boat that was stocked with plenty of fishing gear, and almost every day went out to bait the hooks and cast the lines, but he never caught a living creature. Instead, Captain Rigs had a knack for hooking *everything else* under the water: old tires, boots, lost oars, and discarded wine bottles. Whatever sunken item dwelled in the deep, Captain Rigs had either caught it or would catch it eventually. When he was a young man, his inability to catch fish had almost driven him to madness. He came from a long line of fishermen and dearly loved the life, but as he had grown older, Captain Rigs made peace with his gift. He soon discovered that not only do worthless items live at the bottom of the sea, but also lost treasures. Over the years, Captain Riggins had pulled up a small fortune in gold and other valuables that had once rested peacefully at the bottom of the ocean.

Most were unaware that Captain Rigs was, by far, the wealthiest man in Treadwalla. He ran a modest antique store on Main Street from which he sold, or put on display, various items he had collected. To keep people's suspicion at bay, he kept a few flounder or bass mounted on the walls and occasionally hung around the fish market. But the truth was that his antiques were his only harvest and the fish on the walls were merely plastic.

To see Captain Rigs and Portico standing together was like looking at a bizarre little costume party. Captain Rigs was always decked out in fishing boots, a faded blue captain's hat, a sailor's jacket, and a pipe sticking from his bearded mouth. Portico was dressed like a woodsman and had long, stringy, grey hair surrounding a perfectly untouched clown face. As Emeeca came running, the two men quit their discussion and turned their worried attention to her.

"What seems to be troublin' ya child?" Captain Rigs said as he knelt beside her, concerned.

Emeeca told the pair about all that had happened to her that day and her unfortunate encounter with one Reverend Jonah. While Rigs questioned Emeeca, Portico stood silently and listened. Clown makeup could hide age and even emotion, but as Emeeca told the captain about Reverend Jonah backhanding her, a blaze came alive in Portico's eyes. Without a word, he walked into his shack and returned carrying a shotgun headed for town. Captain Rigs jumped up with his arms raised at the sight of the gun.

"And where in the black abyss do ya think you're goin' with that?" Rigs questioned.

Portico spun around and unthinkingly pointed the gun at Emeeca and Rigs. Waving the weapon wildly he said, "Some men don't know the world at all, no sir! Others jis' get ate up by it. And some think they know every lil' bit so they go 'bout slappin' lil' girls who are differ't than they. Well, I'm gonna go have a chat with Jonah and maybe knock some knowin' out of 'im…and if that don't work, blow a hole in the middle of 'im… jist in case all the knowin' don't wanna come out his ol' head!"

With his hands still raised, Rigs spoke. He was one of the few people who could talk to Portico in a way he understood.

"Ah, right you may be. But what if some of them there men you speak of get a hold of you for blowin' a hole in the 'Right Reverend Jonah' and decide to visit the same on ya? What then will ya do?"

Portico stood for a moment and thought. Then he let out an exasperated grunt and marched back into his cabin. Emeeca and Captain Rigs looked at each other and breathed a sigh of relief. Portico emerged again with a long hunting knife instead.

"Oh I'm not gonna hurt 'im…much," they heard him mutter as he began to march toward town again. Emeeca and Captain Rigs hurried to join him.

To see the three walking down the street side by side would have been quite a sight had it not been for the darkness quickly descending on the town of Treadwalla. Soon they came to the place where Emeeca had her trouble with Reverend Jonah that afternoon. The trio tried the front door of the church, but it was locked. Portico looked both ways and started to pull out his knife to persuade the door. Rigs caught his arm just in time. Instead, he made gestures for them to check behind the building to see if there was another way in.

The church was nestled between two other buildings with a thin alley running alongside of it. At the end of the structure was a tall block wall that surrounded, what appeared to be, a large open space.

Portico hunched down and let Captain Rigs step on his shoulder to scale the wall. He did the same for Emeeca. After he heard her land on the other side, Portico leapt onto the top of the wall like a cat. When he jumped down to join the others, he was greeted by shocked looks. Apparently Portico had more bizarre twists than just his face.

As they peered out, they saw that they were standing in a spacious courtyard with well-groomed gardens, flowerbeds, and small trees scattered throughout. There was a sizable fountain in the heart of the square, surrounded by a cobblestone pathway that branched out and meandered around. Little benches sat along the path. No one would have ever believed that behind the plain looking church, there grew such a splendid oasis.

Just as Portico took a step to head for the building, Reverend Jonah emerged from the back door. The three quickly hid themselves in the shadows behind a twisted olive tree.

Reverend Jonah was pale and sweaty. He looked to be in great pain as his hands fumbled with the buttons on his shirt. He staggered down the two steps from the building into the garden, haltingly making his way to the fountain. As he came to the pool, his knees gave way and he fell to the ground. The three in hiding looked at each other in confusion, but Captain Rigs quickly pointed their attention back. Reverend Jonah had raised himself up on his knees. With his back straight and his hands balancing his weight on his thighs, he began to heave like he was about to empty himself. Suddenly, a bluish white light shot out of Jonah's chest and cast itself on the water falling in the fountain. Strange images began to appear as though on a movie screen.

At first, colors swirled and blended together against the watery backdrop. Then, two distinct figures appeared. The first was a radiant young woman about the age of twenty. She had raven black hair and deep brown eyes. She was dressed with a purple scarf tied around her head, a loose blouse that fell off her shoulder, a ragged skirt, and a sash around her waist. The colors she had chosen should have never been mixed together, but nothing could take away from her beauty. She was a gypsy girl.

The other figure on the watery stage was a young man about her age. He was handsome and dressed in a plain white shirt and tan slacks. He looked like a blank canvas compared to the girl.

As the scene came more into view, it was obvious the two were engaged in an intense discussion. The girl had been crying. She seemed wildly desperate and grasped his hands in hers. The bracelets on her wrists were too many to count and clattered when she moved.

The girl pleaded, "Come away with me! We can live together under my father's shelter. He approves of you. No one can stop us. Please, don't do this!"

The boy pulled his arms away and hung his head.

"No, Alinda. I must stay. There can be no future for us. I have made a terrible mistake. We cannot be together.

My calling is to this town and its people… My family would never understand. I could not live with myself…"

The boy was torn. He was clearly in love with the girl.

The gypsy girl threw her head back in frustration.

"How can I leave you? How can I live after the nights we've spent in each other's arms? You said you loved me. Please come with me!"

The boy turned from her and started to walk away. Tears began to leak from his eyes, but he would not turn back. She cried after him:

"Cursed will be your dwelling of Treadwalla from this day forward, Phineus Jonah. May those you feel so obligated to lead to the light all know strangeness - marks of the strange and twisted life you have chosen for us since we must be apart! Not a day will pass when you won't be reminded that we could have been together!"

The boy stopped in his tracks, horrified. He opened his mouth to speak but nothing came out.

Alinda continued, "You also will bear strangeness, Phineus. Once a year, you will see this moment. For the rest of your life, it will play out before your eyes and remind you of the love you tore apart."

The boy turned to the gypsy girl, but she would not allow herself to look at him anymore. She ran off as the scene faded out of view.

Reverend Jonah was now sobbing on his hands and knees in front of the fountain. Treadwalla had been cursed by a gypsy girl whose love he, Phineus Jonah, had forsaken. What's more, he had spent his life not only living with that knowledge, but being reminded of it again and again in the faces he saw daily who hid their strangeness from his judgmental eyes. Emeeca had her answer.

The trio hiding behind the olive tree stood shocked and still until Captain Rigs could no longer hold back a violent sneeze caused by an unruly moustache hair that had been tickling his nose all day.

Reverend Jonah looked up and saw the three behind the tree. The surprise and embarrassment was unmistakable on his face. He knew they had seen the whole thing. He let go of a small yelp and dashed back inside the church, pulling the door tightly behind him. The trio knew following him would be pointless. They helped themselves over the wall and headed back to the woods.

Emeeca spent the next few days staying close to Portico. Now, knowing what they did, the two sat for many hours putting together little pieces of local lure that might shed light on what they had seen. They wrestled mostly with how Reverend Jonah could have changed from the tender young man they had seen in the water into the hardened Reverend Jonah they knew best. The more they wondered the more questions filled their minds.

One morning, about a week after the incident in Reverend Jonah's garden, Captain Rigs paid a visit to Portico and Emeeca at the cabin.

He was obviously shaken and spoke slowly.

"I was doin' some fishin' last night along the river and caught somethin' I was hopin' I would never find, but found anyhow…Reverend Jonah's body. There was a bounteous stone tied around his ankle to weigh 'im down. Looks like he did it 'imself."

Captain Rigs' speech trailed off as he reverently pulled his cap from his head and clutched it to his heart.

The town of Treadwalla mourned appropriately. School was cancelled for the remainder of the week. The town flag was flown at half-mast. Flowers, notes, and candles were placed on the steps of the church. The church building couldn't hold the whole town, so the funeral service was held the following week at Melody Park. The cemetery sat in a large meadow surrounded by tall pine trees with a quiet brook running through the middle of it.

When Captain Rigs unintentionally fished Reverend Jonah's body out of the water, he cut the stone away from his leg and told the authorities that Jonah must have accidentally drowned. No one questioned the cause of Jonah's death. No matter how it had really happened, everyone seemed at peace in knowing that he was an old man who had finally reached his end.

On a warm summer morning, with strands of light breaking through the tall pine trees around Melody Park, the entire town of Treadwalla turned out to pay their respects, including Emeeca, Portico, and Captain Rigs. Although many were gathered, few had words to say. Reverend Jonah had no remaining relatives or close friends to speak on his behalf. For a man so highly respected among so many, most could only speculate as to Reverend Jonah's real humanity. Finally, as the service was being brought to a close by Judge Willowtree, an unfamiliar voice came from the back of the crowd.

"I'd like to say somethin'…"

It was Portico.

Emeeca's eyes shot open wide. Captain Rigs shook his head and braced for the worst. Gasps and shocked exclamations could be heard from the crowd as Portico made his way toward the finely-crafted box. There were many in Treadwalla who had only heard tales of Portico's existence but had never actually seen the man himself.

As the bizarre figure reached the coffin, he stood there a moment, studying it. Then, as if he were sitting down on a sofa to have a conversation, Portico sat down on the coffin lid and crossed his arms, mumbling something about a "proper seat."

His long hair blew sideways in the gentle breeze as his sad painted face stared out into the stunned crowd.

"I figure there are some folk who don't carry much in life, and what they do carry they got help wit'."

His voice trembled a bit. He had never been in front of so many people. He swallowed and continued.

"Then I figure there are other folk who carry a whole lot and has to do it all by 'em selfs. I reckon things ya wanna say, things ya ought not have done, and things you wish you could do twice again jist sorta get stuck inside a body."

He paused for a moment and looked down at his feet. He then raised his head with a look in his eye like a man who desperately wanted to say something in particular but knew he couldn't.

"I guess in a way you could say that Jonah was a father to this town, to all of us. Musta been mighty hard to carry. Don't know if that's a good thing... when you got somethin' no one knows about... cause of your bein' too scared...Nope, that ain't no good thing sir..."

Portico hopped down from the coffin lid and walked silently through the crowd in the direction of his cabin, alone.

Gradually, the gears of life in Treadwalla began to move again. It was odd to no longer see Reverend Jonah walking down the street, looking so righteously upon everyone else and faithfully holding services in the old church on the corner. For some time, the people pondered what they might do with the now unused building. Although, when it was discovered that a beautiful garden lay behind it, the town council opted to tear the building down and make the courtyard into a public park.

Within a few months of Reverend Jonah's passing, a subtle difference could be felt in the town. It was as if his departure lifted a weight that Treadwalla collectively carried and released a dam of caution it barely managed to maintain.

Little by little, odd people of all shapes, sizes, and nuances began to appear on the streets. Almost daily, bizarre spectacles could be witnessed. Fences and walls that had been built to hide the unexplainable began to come down. The freedom to be *strange* began to spread.

It was a big day and a courageous move when Captain Rigs announced he would change his name to "Collector Rigs" and that he would run for town mayor. An overwhelming majority voted for him as many found his truthfulness about his unique gift refreshing. It was exactly what the town needed.

Emmet Portico continued to live in the woods and do and be what he'd always done and been. He was skeptical at first that anything could change about his town. He seemed weighed down by the fact that he and two others were the only ones who knew the whole truth as to why Treadwalla was such a unique place. He wondered if the curse would be lifted now that Jonah had ended his life or if *odd* would continue to be the norm. With so many questions that only time might or might not answer, Portico remained out of sight. He watched pensively from the shadows until one day, he noticed a distinct difference in the people of Treadwalla. It struck him as noteworthy that people even more unusual than himself were walking around in public. Being moved by such boldness, it wasn't too long until Portico could be seen walking down Main Street on occasion and even humoring a child or two with some tricks he still remembered from the clowns.

Emeeca, the orphan who cast no shadow, remained the smiling, laughing, and inquisitive girl she had always been. She was growing into a young lady. In time, she became what can only be described as the brightest light in the city of Treadwalla. Some even called her "the princess of the peculiar." She was known to everyone and loved by all. Daily she made her rounds through the town, spreading her own brand of sunshine. She delighted in each and every soul. She marveled at their oddities. Emeeca was especially gifted in helping and encouraging those who were just beginning to learn of their own strangeness. And when the sky opened and the gutters of Treadwalla began to fill, often you could catch Rigs, Portico, and Emeeca, dancing with Mrs. Bangarang out in the rain.

Sparrow,

In his newfound way of seeing life F.T. never dreamed some would rather him hang as a heretic than have their version of the truth challenged. Of course he had heard the whispers and knew the penalty for his outrageous claims. But rather like a child, F.T. naively believed he could convert those who were convinced they needed no converting.

In the middle of the night he was awoken from his sleep by cloaked figures. A sack was thrown over his head and his hands were bound. They quickly shoved him out of the parish door and into the back of an ox cart. As the cart rumbled through the dank night air, his captors said not a word.

He sat motionless fighting pangs of fear with prayer. And although he knew the words that could set him free when the time came to be questioned by the bishop, he could no more deny The Great Embrace than deny the sun or moon, or recant the air.

The ox cart jostled him incessantly. The ropes cut into his wrists. The sack covering his head became weighted down by the dew of night. He began to suffocate and a darker darkness took him.

I have heard many of the man's stories, dear Sparrow, wild and vivid, but what I relate to you now may be the most profound for I have no doubt as to its authenticity.

The darkness gave way to a vision: He saw himself surrounded by a large crowd, having just finished entertaining them with a grand story. Hooting and cheering erupted. But as he gazed upon the faces there were none he recognized, nor was their dress something familiar to him. They did not bear the features of his fellow countrymen but were a display of every color and race imaginable - black, brown, yellow, red - wearing the garb of their homeland.

Just then his gaze fell upon a peculiar face. It was foreign to him but yet as familiar as his own reflection. For now F.T. looked into the eyes of the Master, our brother Jesus, standing amongst the crowd. Surely it was the Christ, for as anyone who has every received a vision of the Lord can testify, He has a particularly mischievous smile about Him one never forgets. He looked upon F.T. with a grin and gave a wink.

It was then F.T. heard a voice. It said, "Do not be afraid. For I am in all and they are in me. Tell them, little brother. Tell them your stories."

His transport jolted to a stop, waking him. How much time had gone by he could not tell, but the early morning sun crept through the cloth sack making him sweat. Instantly shouts filled the air. He was pulled unceremoniously from the cart.

A familiar voice cut through the chaos. The sack was yanked from his head, and as his lungs rejoiced in the fresh air so did his eyes as Merrit stood before him. A motley throng of people surrounded her. F.T. saw that he had been brought into the envelope of a dense forest. Yet the makings of a sparse camp, a village, could be seen through the trees. He had often heard suggestions of outcasts and fugitives living free in distant woods. Could this be their dwelling place?

"We knew they would be coming for you soon," Merrit said. "We intercepted a missive that hinted the bishop planned to take you at any time for questioning. We had to get you out without them knowing you'd gone and we knew that you would have never left on your own."

"So, we kidnapped you," interrupted a burly fellow F.T. remembered from the tavern as being an attentive listener to his stories and a rumored outlaw.

"Sorry about the ropes and sack, friend," he added. "It was for your own good."

"We love you," Merritt said with a hopeful expression. "We need you...your stories. Please stay with us."

The prisoner stood before his eager hosts bewildered, for such hospitality he could never have imagined existed.

Limner

The Devil and the Man
Who Did Not Dream

    Maker Starks did not dream. Like most he had hopes and aspirations, but when he drifted off to sleep at night, neither cozy memory, nor nightmare entered his mind. To overhear someone wish another, "sweet dreams," would make him burn with envy. And when he'd catch people speak of the joys of a dreamless slumber, he would shake his head at their ignorance. Maker always slept well, yet it brought him no comfort. Maker Starks did not dream…

    Sipping a steadily warming beer at The Bayou Tavern, Maker sat quietly at the aged oaken bar. The Bayou was Maker's favorite hideout and where he came early each night for a drink after work at the pencil factory. As the evening wore on, the tavern filled with patrons. Maker hated crowds. He would have long since left, but tonight he decided to linger a little longer than usual. What kept him was the most beautiful woman he had ever seen, standing thirty feet away. She was among a small party of friends, casually talking and sipping red wine at a high table. She stood out like a rose in a wheat field. Maker was completely beside himself with desire but he only pined safely from afar, studying her every curve and gesture.

"Gorgeous, isn't she?" a sandpaper voice resonated from the stool beside him.

Maker didn't usually talk to strangers but he couldn't resist muttering a reply.

"Amazing."

The voice continued, "A beautiful creature like that is rare, something the Creator made on one of His better days. It's a damn shame you're at such a disadvantage…"

Maker was shocked for a moment. He wasn't quite sure, but he thought he might have just been insulted. He turned to face the man who had rudely jolted him from his spellbound gaze.

"I beg your pardon?" replied Maker.

The man with the broken voice turned to face him. He wore a small porkpie hat that barely covered a thick mess of curly brown hair. His necktie was loosened and his shirtsleeves rolled up to reveal large forearms covered with bizarre tattoos. His pants, black and baggy, spilled perfectly onto his wing tips. As soon as Maker looked into the stranger's face, he got the feeling he may have hung around too long. The man's eyes were a mesmerizing brown. And in the glow of the dimly lit tavern, they seemed absolutely ablaze with mischief.

"Oh, don't misunderstand me," said the man in the hat. "I mean no disrespect. I didn't mean to imply that if you so *desired* you could not woo or win the heart of such a fair maiden. That is, if you actually *tried* to. But let's face it, you won't. Nor will any other man in here. Beauty like that's almost too painful to look at but somehow, you can't seem to keep your eyes from finding their way back to her again and again. So you'll just sit here and wish like all the rest, but they'll go home tonight, and at the very least, dream of holding her. But you won't…will you, Maker?"

Maker's jaw dropped. He had never told a soul his secret about his inability to dream. He tried to stammer out a rebuttal but the eyes that stared back at him made Maker lower his gaze and admit, "That's right. I don't dream."

"Well, Maker," replied the amber-eyed stranger, "I'm about to make all of your dreams come true, if you'll pardon the expression. You see, I have certain *abilities* at my disposal that would bring you into the ranks of all other men who tread on clouds and dance with angels through the night. Tell me, how else could you discover what's beyond your wildest dreams if you've never even had one? Well, it's time to find out, don't you think? I'll give you the dreams you've always wanted! No charge. No hidden fees or limitations. I'm no stingy genie out of a bottle. Besides, I've always felt three wishes to be poor customer service… All you have to do is sign this little form."

A rolled-up piece of parchment instantly appeared in the man's hand. He laid it on the bar and from thin air produced a black pen with a ruby encrusted ring that encircled its middle.

Maker took the pen and looked down at the parchment. It looked like a legal document with a line at the bottom for his name. Maker went to sign, but then hesitated. He drew back suspiciously.

"What is this, some sort of contract?"

"Oh no…not a contract. It's more of a waiver. It releases me of any, let's say, *liabilities,* in the event you become dissatisfied with my services."

Maker knew better than to sign something he hadn't read, or to enter into a bargain with someone he didn't know. Then, in the mirror behind the bar, he looked up to see her reflection again. She was slowly swaying to the music and looking more beautiful by the minute. He may never learn her name or speak a word to her but if he could dream, he could have her any given night. Maker looked down at the waiver.

"Where do I sign?"

As he left the Bayou, Maker's stomach was a tangled ball of twine. On the one hand, the man had promised his dreams would begin that very night. On the other hand, Maker was fairly certain he had just made a deal with the devil.

The following morning, Maker was late for work. It took every ounce of his willpower to get out of bed. His dreams had been so magical, he almost believed one night made up for a lifetime without them. The beauty from the Bayou had been the star of each and every one of his fantasies, romantic and erotic. It was absolutely divine, and he didn't want it to end.

As soon as his shift at the pencil factory was over that day, Maker skipped the tavern and headed straight home. He had never been one to go to bed early, but like a child with a brand new toy, Maker was eager to explore his newfound world.

He was in bed shortly after supper. The anticipation of what may lie ahead kept him awake for longer than he had hoped. But once he began to drift off, his shuttle of dreams quickly appeared and moved him along until morning.

Maker's Bayou Beauty did not make a second appearance, but he hardly noticed. He was much too taken with the most vivid fancies a man might possibly conceive of. He flew like a bird above the clouds. He was a fish in a tropical blue ocean - not to mention a popular author, a brave knight, and a millionaire playboy. He cured diseases and told his boss what he really thought of him.

At the turn of a month, Maker was a different man. Although his sleep was less restful than before, he would not trade his new kaleidoscope of dreams for the world. There was a new spring in his step and an incurable smile painted on his face. He found his mundane employment to be much more bearable now that his nights were filled with adventure. Maker was finally happy and rarely gave a thought to just how all these fortunate dreams had come to him or parchments he had signed.

The night the trouble began, the evening had started out like any other. He had come home from work, eaten a light dinner, read the paper, and gone directly to bed. The extraordinary had become routine to him. Of course his dreams were always new and exciting, but at least now he could fall asleep without first lying awake in restless anticipation, wondering what the night held in store.

It was sometime around dawn when Maker's Bayou Beauty returned. He had dreamt of her at least three or four times since he had signed the strange parchment. Each time, the visions of her left him weak from pleasure and eager for another visit. Tonight, however, she seemed distant and cold, rejecting Maker's advances. She bore a look of disdain toward him and walked away, leaving him desperately calling after her. Maker felt his heart break as he opened his eyes to the harsh morning sun.

The day brought an uneasy feeling. He didn't know what to make of this new dream. The man at the bar had never mentioned bad dreams. Could these have been in the contract he had so quickly and carelessly signed? Maybe the dream was merely an aberration or a glitch in the system. He finally reasoned that in a lifetime of perfect tomatoes, you're bound to come across a rotten one once in a while. He went home from work, performed his nightly ritual, and got ready for bed.

Disturbing dreams crowded in. He was back at school and handed a pop quiz he hadn't studied for. He was running away from something but his legs wouldn't move properly. He argued with his boss, and searched desperately for an item he had lost, but he couldn't remember what it could be.

Like watching a close friend slowly die of a wasting disease, Maker could hardly bring himself to admit what he knew deep inside was happening: Something had gone terribly wrong. His dreams were turning into nightmares.

Within a fortnight, hideous faces began to peer into the windows of his mind. He was beaten with thunderous blows he could neither see nor repel. He was naked, cold, and alone. His face and hands burned in a fire he couldn't pull away from. Instead of flying, he was falling.

On the hour, Maker was jolted awake, drenched in sweat. His neighbors began to complain about the blood-curdling screams erupting nightly from his bedroom window.

The waking world that had been a tolerable annoyance until he could return to his dreams now became a refuge from his nightly terrors. Maker no longer rushed home after work. Instead, he found himself lingering at the tavern until closing time, until he would be forced to return home and go to sleep.

There was no relief. After waking countless times during the night, Maker would rise every morning thoroughly exhausted. His bedroom had become a torture chamber, his bed the rack. Maybe sleep was overrated. He decided to avoid it altogether.

For four days straight, Maker stayed awake. Although free from his nightmares, how long could he go on denying his body the rest it demanded? It was only a matter of time before his brain would begin to deteriorate. He was dozing at his job and slurring his words when he spoke. Walking down the street without moving sideways into walls or oncoming traffic became a chore. He began to hallucinate.

Unlike his nightmares, Maker's hallucinations were much tamer, although socially awkward. His coworkers would find him at his post, staring off into nowhere, nattering away to no one. The furniture began to move on its own and the walls began to teem with roaches.

It was in one such hallucination that Maker saw the man in the hat. He knew by now that it truly was the devil that had persuaded him to sign the parchment that night at the bar. No one else could create nightmares with such twisted plotlines. Maker was walking down the street when the devil suddenly appeared walking toward him.

Maker cut him off slurring, "Yoooouuuu!"

The devil looked baffled at first. Then a knowing grin spread across his face.

"Ah, yes, Maker Starks… How goes it ol' boy? Enjoying your dreams?"

"You lied to me. You s-set m-me up!"

"Oh no," replied the devil, looking hurt. "I see you are experiencing a bit of buyer's remorse, but I assure you that I never lied to you or set you up. It was all in the parchment I seem to remember you were in quite a hurry to sign. It's all in there, Maker. I write the stories. I recruit the actors. I produce and direct. I have total creative control. Your signature provided the movie house that I see you are now trying to close…" The devil clicked his tongue, leaned in close and hellishly whispered in Maker's ear, "How long do you think you can go without sleep, Maker? I have some new pieces I'm sure you are going to find absolutely hair-raising."

"I want out!" shouted Maker. "I want to stop dreaming. No more!"

"Ah, Maker, Maker, Maker…I'm sorry, but I can't do that. The contract you signed is binding. I just can't throw it aside. Besides, you of all people should know that to stop would hurt my artistic soul. I'm a *creator* Maker, not a *destroyer*; a giver, not a taker. Anyway, it's been fun Maker, but I really must be going…pleasant dreams!" said the devil as he tipped his hat and started to stroll away.

Maker reached out to grab him but missed by a great deal. He swung with all of his might, fists flailing in the air, but his arms only passed through the devil like he wasn't there at all. The devil walked through him and crossed the street.

Maker chased after him screaming.

"You liar!! You cheat!! Come back here!! Make them stop!!"

Amidst his screams, Maker could hear a chorus of other cries and a horn growing louder. The blast dispersed the trance. To his horror, he found himself standing in the middle of a busy street with cars flying past. From the sidewalks, people were pointing and yelling at him. He fled the scene and made his way to his last refuge.

The Bayou was mostly deserted. A few regulars littered the dimly lit room while a young couple occupied the pool table near the corner. Maker sat at the bar with his head hung low and his nose dangerously close to drowning him in his pint. Dark, sunken circles rounded the eyes on his pale face. His head swam and his stomach churned. His clothes felt like tightened burlap. He drifted in and out of sleep as oblivion called. If the bartender hadn't known him, he would have had Maker tossed out for being too drunk, but it was a slow night so he let the poor soul be. Maker had just jerked out of another fit of sleep when a stranger walked to the barstool beside him and sat down.

He was slightly older than Maker with dark hair and glasses. He wore khaki colored pants and a loose fitting button-down shirt. When he ordered his drink, Maker could detect a thick southern accent. The man had a jovial air about him - the type of person who never met a stranger. From his sleepless haze, Maker could hear him chatting up the bartender, an annoyance he was beyond the point to do anything about.

"You don't look so good, son," said the man turning to Maker. "You look like you could use a few months of shut-eye."

Maker was prepared to say something snide but the stranger's voice was so warm and paternal that it disarmed him. Maker turned to the man with tears in his eyes, but all he could get out was a weak, "uh-huh."

The man smiled back and said, "Well, my bus doesn't arrive on the corner for about another hour. I assume there's a story behind why you look so bad, so I'm all ears. I love a good story."

Maker felt so ill with despair that he poured out his tale to the stranger. The man listened quietly, taking small sips of dark ale with the expression of someone who'd heard the exact same story a million times yet didn't mind hearing it again.

When he had finished, the man looked at him with a pained expression.

"I'm sorry, son. I'm sorry that had to happen to you. Seems like that scoundrel always knows right where to poke ya, and when he finds it, he just keeps digging away at it. He's fiendish like that."

"You *know* him?" Maker's dead eyes lit up in shock.

"Oh, I know that little dirt bag. I've had my own share of run-ins with him over the years. He's like ants in the kitchen. Once you get 'em, they're hell to get rid of. And it only takes a crumb or two left on the counter to have 'em come charging right back in. Yeah, I know him…"

For the first time in months, Maker began to feel something almost like hope rise up inside of him. If this stranger had tangled with the devil before and lived to tell the story, maybe there was a chance for him after all.

"Do you know anything about…about his contracts? Is there a w-way to beat him? Is there a l-loophole somewhere?" Maker was so desperate he almost grabbed the stranger by his collar.

The stranger just sat and looked back at him. He knew the answer, but he obviously wasn't going to give it away for free.

"Please!" begged Maker. "Please help me! I'm inches away from falling asleep again and seeing the most terrifying things no…no person could even imagine. What's more, he has me bound to a contract that I know will f-forfeit my very soul to him. Please! He'll drag…drag me to hell!"

The man looked back at Maker with a funny look on his face.

"Drag you to hell?" the stranger said. "Why would he have to do that, son? He's already got you. You're *in* hell. You should know by now that hell isn't just a destination. Hell can be livin' in your own skin, or in your case – livin' in your dreams."

"Then there's no hope!" Maker sighed. "I'm lost. My soul is lost. What a fool I've been…" Utterly crushed, Maker turned back around to face his beer and hang his head.

"Have you ever seen an Alfred Hitchcock film?" said the stranger.

Maker knew for sure his fate was sealed. The stranger had moved on and turned the conversation to lighter subjects. Maker had only seen pictures of the rotund balding man he recalled in black and white. He was not a fan of movies.

"Um…n-no," mumbled Maker.

"Hitchcock was a genius when it came to film," said

the stranger. "In his era, he was by far the most intense storyteller around. But there was something about Hitchcock's movies that set him apart from the rest. You see, Hitchcock fancied himself an actor. If you watch his pictures carefully, you'll find him in every one. Somehow he always found a way to get himself into the script. Most of the time, he appears in a small cameo. He's a man walking down the street, or a doorman in a hotel, or even a bartender who'll hand the leading man a drink. Average moviegoers never noticed him because they weren't looking for him, but he was always there…somewhere."

Maker was only half-listening to the stranger. Who cared if Hitchcock appeared in his own movies? He had much larger issues to deal with than meaningless movie trivia. Then it hit him as he remembered his last exchange with the devil. What was it he had said?

…I write the stories. I recruit the actors. I produce and direct…

"You mean the devil…the devil is in my dreams?" Maker sputtered. "But how? I've n-never seen him! I guess I never looked…Where could he hide?"

The stranger smiled mischievously.

"Now you're catching on! But you didn't hear that from me, nor did you hear that his contracts read more like the rules found in children's games like duck-duck-goose, tag, or even…*hide and seek.* Once you find who's hiding…well… the game's over, isn't it?"

The stranger was pulling out his wallet to pay the bartender.

"So I have to find the devil in my dreams…and then,

and then what?" Maker shouted at the stranger's back as he headed for the door.

The stranger turned around and smiled.

"You'll know what to do when you find him. No matter how it turns out though, make sure you give that lil' rat bastard a swift kick in the ass for me. And tell him, 'hello,' from Baxter."

With a wink and smile he pushed open the door and disappeared.

Maker threw a wad of money on the bar and quickly made for home. He could barely walk, but a newfound quest for freedom drove him on. He staggered down the street and finally made it to his front door. At last, he could get some sleep, even if it was filled with nightmares - and, if he was lucky, find the devil lurking in the shadows.

Sleep came to Maker the moment his head hit the pillow. Horrors immediately came crashing in. Flaming visions of sadness, pain, and death were flying at him from all directions. Maker was about to lose himself to sheer terror but something reminded him why he was choosing such torture. He had to find the devil. He had to find the devil's hiding spot and stop him.

He scanned the terrifying landscape for any sign of the devil's face, but it was like trying to find loose change on the freeway during rush hour. Maker's mind was being overrun. He burst awake in a pool of sweat.

It was six in the morning. It was almost time for work, but work would have to wait. He had to return to his dreams and find the devil. Once more, Maker laid his head on his pillow and drifted quickly back to sleep.

What awaited him were longer and more sorrowful scenes. He dreamt of losing his first real pet, a dog named Snoops. He felt the overwhelming pain of loss. As he looked around the empty kitchen where Snoops used to eat and sleep, he saw no one. He ran outside and surveyed his old neighborhood, but no one could be seen. The houses were all dark and empty.

Hopelessness crowded in. How could he find the devil in dreams that the devil himself had authored? He suddenly felt silly and stupid for trying to beat the Prince of Darkness at his own game.

His self-loathing launched yet another childhood dream: Report card day. Maker met his father's cold eyes. Over the past month he had been reintroduced to the man's face more than a few times.

Fourth grade had not been a good year for Maker. His teacher seemed to hate him and he had trouble making friends. He dreaded bringing home his report card. It had to be signed by a parent. Unfortunately, Maker's father saw the report before his mother and studied it carefully.

"What are you some sort of idiot?" yelled his father. "I work my fingers to the bone to support this family and all the gratitude you can muster is to bring home C's and D's every quarter? How are you going to survive in this world, Maker? You certainly won't be a rocket scientist, that's for sure! Say so long to your stupid dreams. You'll be lucky if you get to see the world at all from riding on the back of a trash truck!"

His father believed shame was an important tool when it came to the raising of children and wielded it like a

Samurai sword whenever Maker was concerned.

Maker felt the heavy blanket of humiliation fall upon his ten-year-old shoulders. He knew what was coming next: a beating to drive every word from his father home. Maker bowed his head as tears of rage and fear began to gather.

His father was still carrying on.

"To think that a retard like you came from my blood is an absolute embarrassment. I guess I'd better sign this piece of crap and get it over with! Run up to your room and wait for me." His father grabbed a pen and furiously scribbled his signature.

As Maker turned to scurry up to his room something caught his eye. A beam of light reflected off the pen in his father's hand to reveal a ruby-encrusted center. Maker froze in his tracks. He had seen that pen before, but where?

Maker shook himself of the shame and fear. He felt his courage rise.

"You!" Maker shouted.

His father looked up from his writing.

"What are you talking about boy? Go up to your room. I'll be up soon enough to finish our discussion."

Maker would not be put off this time.

"It was you who had me sign the contract! You lied to me. You fooled me into letting you control my dreams! You ruined my best memories! You used my mind as a stage for your nightmares!"

"What are you talking about boy? You'd better run along before I decide to give you something extra!"

"You're not my father! You're the devil! That's *your* pen. I know it. I found you. Get out!"

136

His father was looking back at him now, eye to eye. No longer was Maker a child, but standing tall as a man.

"Maker…" said his father in a slightly less hostile tone. The devil was beginning to break character. "Maker, do you *really* think you can stop dreaming by simply throwing me out? This isn't hide and seek, you fool. This is *my* show. Now go to your room!"

Hearing the devil speak through his father's voice made Maker shiver, but he steeled himself.

"No," Maker said defiantly. "This is *my* mind. These are my dreams. Get out now!"

The devil cocked his head in a strange way and grinned toothily back at him.

Maker was desperate now. He was close. He grabbed the pen out of the devil's hand and began to move toward him raising it like a knife. The devil started to back away, slowly.

"Now, Maker, calm down… Do you really want to go back to having no dreams at all? Don't you remember what a miserable state that was?"

Maker continued to inch closer.

A higher pitch took over the devil's voice.

"It was *me* who gave you the girl! I gave you the adventures! Sure, I may have gotten carried away…but you're a *freak* without me, Maker! Do you hear me? A pitiful freak! You and your dreamless inhuman mind! You *need* me! You need my work! My art!"

Maker plunged forward with one great thrust and stabbed the devil through the chest. The encrusted pen stuck out by only an inch as blood immediately began to spread over his father's white button shirt.

At first, Maker was terrified that he might have made a mistake as his father reeled and swayed with the pen sticking out of his heaving body. Then his father's dark eyes began to change to bright amber. He began to flicker like a television screen on the fritz. Each time he disappeared and reappeared, he looked more and more like the man in the porkpie hat. Soon the devil stood before him, unmasked, with the pen still sticking out of his chest.

The devil looked at Maker with a regretful smile.

"Now I'll have to find another theatre..."

Like a warehouse of fireworks bursting into flames, the devil exploded into a million pieces of light. The blast threw Maker back through the front door, sending fragments of glass in all directions. Maker felt his head hit the concrete walkway as a halo of searing pain wrapped around his skull. Everything went black...

Maker awoke three days later. He knew he had certainly lost his job, but all he really wanted at the moment was to get something to eat and lie back down. When he did, Maker once more drifted off to sleep. He awoke sometime during the small hours of morning. He looked carefully at his alarm clock and realized that he had not dreamt of anything. It was over. Maker Starks did not dream.

House Money

By the time the casino's operating director arrived, a crowd had already gathered to take in the horror. The flashing lights of emergency vehicles lit the scene like a stage show. Atop the crushed roof of what was once a beautifully restored 1948 Lincoln Continental, lay the twisted puppet-like body of a middle-aged man in a white suit. The costly threads were already rapidly absorbing the thick crimson fluid that oozed from every imaginable, and not so imaginable, place.

Police were urgently shoving the crowds back and taping off the area. The operating director only needed one glance to piece together what must have happened. He gasped.

"Oh my God, Jerry!"

The private jet that flew high above the clouds was now beginning to make its final descent. As he sat comfortably in the plush leather seat, Jerry Quince closed his eyes and drank in the moment, savoring the champagne he had been sipping. After years of funding his own trips to Vegas from his home in Phoenix, it hardly seemed possible that this tab would fall to someone else. The Grand Hotel & Casino had finally taken notice of his talents and had graciously offered to compensate his entire trip. Everything would be included: food, beverages, a top floor suite, and twenty-five thousand dollars in house money.

Since dropping out of high school, Jerry had bounced around from job to job. He'd sold cars, managed fast food restaurants, framed houses, and even done a short stint as a bar manager. Nothing ever lasted very long. He was restless by nature. After a year or two of doing the same old thing, the excitement would wear off, sending him on a search for the next intriguing way to make money. Unfortunately, the same pattern held true for the women in his life. He'd been married twice and suffered scores of failed relationships in between. By now, he was self-aware enough to concede that it was his curious nature and almost foolhardy determination that made his relationships difficult. He and his first wife, Elaine, were fresh out of high school when they drove to Vegas and got married in a small wedding chapel that was open all night. Her parents had disowned her for eloping. As for his family, no one really cared much what he did with his life so long as he was doing it for himself and wasn't asking for any handouts. Within a year of saying "I do," they divorced and went their separate ways as friends. It was Jerry's second wife, Janice, however, who became the antidote against ever walking down the aisle again. After the first two years, they fought constantly. It usually had to do with either sex or money, both of which Janice claimed Jerry couldn't come by legitimately if his life depended on it. Unable to cope with his running around and gambling, Janice left and the marriage ended in an ugly way after five years.

Gambling for Jerry had always been a way to make

quick, easy money or unwind from a stressful week. On occasion, he would be invited along on a weekend trip to Vegas with his buddy, Juan. He and Juan lived it up while in Vegas, and playing poker or hitting the slot machines was only a small part of the entire package. But obsession's grasping hands finally took hold one night after Jerry decided to linger at the blackjack table. Somehow, he had come away with two thousand dollars more than what he'd come to town with. After that, Jerry started making his own trips to Vegas. Heading up north, once a year on a whim, quickly became an every weekend affair.

It was his unnatural luck and unique fashion style that had caught the eye of the operating manager, Warren. Jerry always wore a white suit and a broad smile when he'd come to gamble at The Grand. People would crowd around him at the tables to watch him place bets and predict how the cards would shake out. The less fortunate always stood close, hoping his luck would rub off.

After a year of taking the casino for more money than it ever could have expected, Jerry was personally invited to The Grand's High Roller Weekend by Warren himself. He was being included in the ranks of greatness. It felt good to be noticed. Finally, he had found his niche.

As the jet touched down, Jerry felt a lightning flash of anticipation go through him. Tonight, he would be unstoppable. Tonight, he would be a god.

A white limo, courtesy of the Grand Hotel, greeted him as he stepped out of the airport's glass doors into the rapidly cooling Vegas night. Waiting inside were more leather-upholstered seats, champagne, and a promotional brochure from the casino. If this was how the rich and famous lived, Jerry wanted in. Finally, the limo driver opened his door. He stepped out onto The Strip and made his way into the rotunda. Meanwhile, three beautiful women standing nearby eyed him hungrily. Forget the fame - riches would probably do just fine.

After checking himself in, dinner was the first priority before a full night of winning. The Grand had four different restaurants to choose from. Jerry picked the most expensive one. Everything was free: lobster, caviar, prime rib, whatever he wanted. Sitting alone at his private table, he noticed people glancing at him from over the top of their menus. He knew they were intrigued. He fancied they were talking about him, wondering who he could be, and guessing at his identity. He made sure to order the most expensive dishes he could find. The servers called him "Mr. Quince." It was almost like living in a dream. And to think, the evening hadn't even begun yet.

To say that his suite was top-notch would have been modest. The floors were marble, the fixtures were cast in gold, and all of the furniture shone in leather. If there was a size beyond "King" for a bed, it was what he would be sleeping on sometime tonight, hopefully with company. There was a hot tub in the center of the room that would have qualified for a small pool back in Phoenix. But what really made the suite was the view. As he pulled back the dark purple curtains, the Vegas lights danced and twinkled up at him like a billion beckoning stars.

The view could wait. It was time to play; time to win.

Jerry showered and meticulously groomed himself. Tonight, people would finally learn his name. Within hours, he would make his mark and begin his meteoric rise to greatness. After this, maybe he'd quit gambling altogether or continue on and become the highest grossing blackjack player in the world. Maybe he'd buy a casino someday.

Still musing over the possibilities, he pulled on his pants and donned his white suit. What had once been the height of fashion decades ago had made its resurgence. Jerry sported it like a man who was in control, proud and strong. The white suit wasn't for just anyone. You had to have just the right look and swagger to wear it. He smirked at himself in the full-length mirror as he adjusted his coat sleeves. He was almost six feet tall. His thick dark hair and sharp features all accentuated a large, pointed nose that brought him up just short of handsome.

Within minutes, Jerry found the casino a beehive of activity. The sound of slot machines and roulette wheels buzzed in the air. The floor was packed with people of all sorts, blundering about with wild eyes, desperately scanning for their next chance to win a fortune. They gathered at the tables like flies to old meat. Some played while others just watched.

Jerry headed straight for his favorite blackjack table, but was intercepted by Warren before he could reach it. The savvy manager shook his hand and asked if he was enjoying himself. Jerry liked Warren. He was a man in his late fifties with grey hair and fashionable glasses that hung on a string around his neck. It was Warren's job to know the high rollers and make sure they were treated properly. Jerry politely gushed about having the time of his life while keep-ing one eye on the open chair at the table. He was itching to get started. Warren could sense that Jerry had his mind on more pressing matters and left it at, "If you need anything, just find me."

As Jerry approached the table, he felt almost as though he were walking through the door of his own home. Blair was dealing tonight. She was an attractive woman in her late forties with a bright smile and dark red hair. She wore rings on almost all of her long fingers, one of which was a massive diamond that was hard to miss. Jerry won-dered if she really was engaged or just wore it to keep men from hitting on her.

She smiled as he came to the table and greeted him.

"Hey! Look who it is! How ya' doin', Jerry? Come to soak us for more money tonight?"

Like Warren, it was her job to be friendly and make sure the customers felt special. She was good at what she did. She had a sultry rasp in her voice and a twinkle in her eye that always made Jerry feel good. The players at the table looked up at him warily from their piles of chips. Jerry made certain to let them know he was the real deal - that a pro was now entering the fray. He handed Blair his voucher for chips. As she counted out his stacks, he immediately threw her a big tip. He made it a policy to always tip his dealers well. Blair called for bets and dealt the cards.

The first hour, Jerry just couldn't settle in. It seemed no matter how hard he tried, he just couldn't string together enough wins. One step forward, two steps back. He busted twice for every winning hand. But as his second hour at the table approached, he could feel his luck starting to roll in like a slow moving weather front. He was doubling down more and more. Within two hours, he was up big. His twenty-five grand had turned into seventy-five with no signs of stopping. Tonight, he would make history.

By the turn of the next half hour, Jerry was cruising at one million dollars. The pulsating high of success flooded his senses. He ordered everyone at the table drinks, not to mention those who had now crowded around to witness the spectacle. He was a winner. He was unstoppable.

It was somewhere near twelve o'clock when a short man with a stringy beard, sunglasses, and a bolo tie approached the table. He spoke in a pinched Texan drawl and paid little attention to anyone else as he was quickly introduced to the game. Jerry recognized him from the high stakes poker table on the other side of the room and had seen him around the casino once or twice before. Blair called the man "Junior."

Within a short time, the weather front of Jerry's luck seemed to be moving on. In all of his time playing, he had never seen the likes of Junior's luck - thunderstruck that anyone, including himself, could be dealt more aces and faces. Junior must have been some kind of fortune-teller to predict what was coming. Jerry was growing frustrated and jealous. He had intended to be the big dog in the house tonight, but his chips were steadily migrating across the table to the poker player. He could feel it slipping.

Back at fifty thousand, Jerry knew that he was failing. He would just have to play through it. People were beginning to walk away to watch other games. It had become impossible to string anything together anymore. He loosened his tie and unbuttoned his shirt after ordering another drink. He must have drawn twenty lines in the sand where the losing would stop and the winning would begin again. But each time he drew another line, the cards would erase it. He was sliding and couldn't stop.

One bad decision after another had Jerry growing more and more desperate and angry. With each busted hand, his frustration crept closer to the surface. After losing to Blair for what seemed like the millionth time, he finally lost it.

"Would you give me a break?" he screamed.

Blair returned his plea with a strange look. Jerry had never been one to raise his voice. Her eyes met with the pit boss standing nearby. Jerry quickly apologized. He lowered his head, gazed at his remaining chips, and crawled back into his own private hell.

It was now two in the morning and Jerry was down to three thousand after only a few hours. His head was swimming, and he knew he had to walk away. He couldn't lose it all. It was over. He reluctantly stood from his seat, gathered his chips, and tapped out of the game.

Junior had long since gone after only playing for an hour and cleaning up. Jerry realized now that Junior had the right idea and that he had stayed too long.

Stepping outside of the casino to get some fresh air was a good idea. But as Jerry leaned against the wall and watched the parade of people strolling along The Strip, it seemed like they all knew him. They all knew he was the one that had tried to swim with the big fish, only to get eaten in the end. It was as if everyone walking by was laughing at him. They knew he was a loser. He could feel their contempt. He could sense their hatred as he turned it in on himself. It burned like fire in his chest.

Jerry knew what he had to do. He could still prove them all wrong. There was still a chance. He had three grand left. He could turn it around. The fresh air rejuvenated him and reminded him that true winners never quit. Crashing was not an option. He raised his head like a fighter, beaten to a pulp, but too proud to throw in the towel. Clenching his jaw, he marched back into The Grand, more determined than ever.

The casino, unlike the last time he had entered, felt like a tomb: foreign, dark, and uninviting. Finding his old table again, Jerry was startled to see a new dealer had taken over.

"Where's Blair?" he said.

The dealer informed him that Blair's shift had ended, and if he wanted to join the game, he needed to hurry and place his bet. This new dealer seemed unfriendly and cold, not at all like Blair. Fumbling for his chips, Jerry quickly sat down and placed a one hundred dollar marker on the table.

Within forty-five minutes he had been wrung out again. It seemed the cards had run out of mercy. Every hand was another defeat, but he couldn't stop himself now. He had come too far. If he could just get a win, it may launch him into a new streak of luck.

Exhaling loudly and running his fingers through his hair, he slammed his last two chips on the table.

The cards were as low as they had been all night: a

two of clubs and a four of spades. The dealer was showing a jack of diamonds. Jerry knew he would need at least two hits if he was going to come out on top. He was the only one at the table now, just him and the surly dealer. The first hit was another low card, the three of hearts. Instinctively Jerry motioned for another hit. This time a queen showed her face. The smile that had quit him a few hours ago returned. He had come as close to breaking as he possibly could. It would take the devil's own luck to beat him now. He watched intently as the dealer flipped his hidden card over to reveal the king of hearts.

"I'm sorry sir," the dealer muttered, mildly sympathetic.

Jerry couldn't speak or move. He watched as the dealer addressed a new player that had just come to the table. It was as if he was having a nightmare in slow motion, yet everything was happening too fast. This couldn't be. This was not how it was supposed to happen.

By the time he caught up with the moment, the exasperated dealer was informing him that he could no longer sit at the table unless he was planning on playing. But Jerry was out of chips, out of money, and out of the game.

"Where's Blair? I want to see Blair!" he yelled.

The explanation from the other side of the table was drowned out as Jerry kept getting louder. Heads began to turn as he stammered frantically, "You're not my dealer! I want my dealer! You cheated me! I'm not a loser! You're the loser! I need more chips!"

The pit boss made his way over to the table where Jerry had now kicked over his stool and was pointing his finger, yelling at the dealer. It only took a touch from the large man's hand to startle him back to his senses. Without any struggle, Jerry backed away and ran wildly through the crowd toward the elevator doors that were just closing as he entered. He shrank into the corner and prayed that when the doors opened again, this would all have been a dream - that his night had only just begun. Soon, he would emerge from his steel cocoon to find the casino once more alive and Blair's friendly face welcoming him.

Back in his suite the hollow sound of the door closing behind him drove his despair even deeper. He felt alone and empty. Luckily, the mini-bar was fully stocked. He was already well past his limit, but he no longer cared.

As he sat on the edge of the bed and worked through his second glass of scotch, the ugly voices from the street began to speak to him again, bending his mind and pulling him lower. He finally acknowledged what he really was: a loser. He was a high school dropout who should have stayed in school, a complete failure, and a fool to even try. No wonder Blair had left the table. They all leave, and for good reason... Elaine and Janice. It was all a waste. That's all he had amounted to, a waste.

Tears streamed down his face as he staggered around his room. He beat his fists against the wall and kicked over a glass table near the kitchenette, only to have it shatter into a million pieces. Fearful that he would be caught and charged for the damages, he backed away from the mess like it was a rattlesnake ready to strike.

He bolted out of his room and staggered down the

hall. There was a glowing exit sign at the end of the corridor. Jerry made for the light, pushed open the cold steel door, and found himself confronted with steps. Instead of going down, he fled upwards.

After two flights, Jerry came to another door that opened onto the roof of the Grand Hotel. He forced it loose and found himself looking out into the cold, dark Vegas night. Swallowing hard he walked forward like a soldier. At thirty paces, he had come to the edge and stared down at the ever-burning lights of The Strip. What once seemed to him like an oasis now resembled a swarming sea of humanity; humanity, scurrying around, looking for the same things he had always wanted: a little piece of happiness, however fleeting it may be. Like grasping a handful of sand too tightly, the best things had slipped through his fingers because he was no good. No one would miss him. No one would care or notice if he ended it.

Leaning slightly forward, Jerry jerked back reflexively as the pull of the earth made his stomach jump.

One step would be all it would take. It would be over quick. It wouldn't even hurt. Then he could be free. Free from stupid pursuits and disappointments… free from the world and the failure he knew he was…just one step.

The wind in his face made the tears in his eyes streak backward into his ears. The black hard earth was racing at him with surprising speed. Gravity had a sobering effect as Jerry was once again reminded why he was hurtling to his end. He had lost one million dollars. Then, with striking clarity, seconds before impact, one final thought intruded into his resigned psyche bringing a sad smile: all this time, he had been playing with house money.

Sparrow,

As the first flames touched the edge of his parish they had no idea he was watching from the edge of the forest. And as the tendrils of smoke began to rise, he wondered if they had any inkling of the lifetime of work they now so casually were destroying. He winced as small explosions began to erupt - the fire having now undoubtedly reached where he kept his stores of homemade ale. That, however, was only a small part of the reason they had come. His love of such common pleasures was merely an excuse they had nailed to the door of his home and house of worship before putting it to the torch. No, what they hated him for, what they despised the most, and why he must not be allowed to live were the stories...

The bishop had called them scandalous and heretical. What he was teaching ordinary people was an affront to accepted doctrine. Apparently, telling common people that God was actually in them, that the acceptance and love of Christ were already the most certain and fundamental elements of their lives which bound all together...well, it was just not the sort of teaching that made men of power and authority comfortable.

But it was too late. The people had already caught on to the stories. Even the children were reciting them as they played in the streets. What he had shared in every tavern and welcoming home for miles around had taken root. They could burn his parish and label him an outlaw for the company he kept, but they could not snuff out the truth, for it was already written deep in the heart of all.

Ducking back further into the cover of the wood he raised his hood, turned, and began making his way back to his new home amongst those who had the courage to believe - the courage to believe that God was indeed good, and therefore the lover of all! The stories had confirmed it, and the stories must continue...and so they have.

Limner

Bobby's Rock

Slowly shuffling around, Bob Darcy found the piece of oak trim he'd been looking for and made his way back over to the table saw that sat in the middle of the workshop. Nearly the size of a small house, the detached garage was where Bob spent most of his time. Today, he was in the middle of finishing a set of cabinets he'd been working on. It was early autumn. The multicolored leaves were now drifting lightly to the ground - fireworks in reverse. A minty breeze blew through the trees, and although the sun shone brightly, the day was crisp. Bob loved this time of year the most. Happiness meant flinging the shop doors open wide and playing country music on a beat-up radio. Over his black tee shirt, he wore a light flannel jacket. Sawdust now peppered his clothes along with his closely trimmed white beard that accentuated his grayish blue eyes. He had just turned seventy.

The workshop was a tangled bird's nest of tools, scrap wood, cans, metal boxes, and other random items he had collected over the years. Still, a narrow path wound its way around the dusty shelves and cluttered floor. A skilled carpenter and builder for most of his life, Bob now spent his time fishing down by the lake or doing small projects for people who still appreciated true craftsmanship. The cabinets would be done either today or tomorrow, depending on how quickly he felt like being finished with them. Being methodical by nature, he preferred to take his time. He loved to build - it relaxed him. His rough hands proved his devotion to his craft with hardly a fingertip that hadn't been permanently disfigured by countless hammer blows.

With a short, loud cry of the blade, Bob had just finished cutting the trim when a white pickup truck appeared outside. Frank Brennan was Bob's junior by twenty years, but the private contractor enjoyed spending time with the old man. Bob had more tools than most hardware stores and was always willing to lend them out as long as they were returned in a timely manner.

Hopping down out of his truck, Frank resembled a younger version of Bob. Slightly balding on top, he wore dark hair that came to just above his shoulders with a long beard to match. Frank was from Delta, a small town up north. It was far enough away for Bob to consider it "country." He jokingly called Frank "Hillbilly."

"What brings you down here, Hillbilly?" Bob shouted with a smile as he turned to put the piece of wood down and dust off his hands.

"Hey Bobby! I just come down to maybe borrow that pipe wrench you said you had."

Looking around and shaking his head, Bob replied, "Hum, yeah I got it… somewhere. I gotta clean this place up someday."

Frank laughed as he stepped inside the garage and absorbed the scene. Scattered tools and trinkets filled him with friendly envy. The mingled smells of fresh-cut oak, sweat, rust, and motor oil hung in the air. It was the exact look and smell Frank imagined would fill his own work-shop someday. But like an artist's paint-splotched studio or a mechanic's grimy garage, he knew that time's wrinkled hands only imparted such well-worn places.

The old man walked toward a cooler tucked under one of the worktables.

"Can I buy you a beer?" said Bob bending over the sacred store of beverages. Frank's eyes twinkled back.

"Sure thing, Bobby," Frank was never one to turn down a cold beer.

Reaching into the cooler, Bob pulled out two icy cans with one massive hand and offered one to his guest.

"So what are you up to today, Hillbilly?" said the old man, making his way over to two lawn chairs set by the door. Bob slowly sank into one of them and propped his feet up on a small object covered with an old sheet. Frank came over, plopped down and began to vent about the plumbing problems at his house - how his wife was threatening to leave if he didn't get it fixed this weekend. Bob just smiled. Contractors were all alike. They would run around, fixing and building for just about everyone but their own home and family. He knew...he was the same way.

The light conversation meandered. Bob enjoyed hearing about Frank's jobs and the progress he was making or the problems the clients were causing him. After more than forty years of dealing with the same troubles, it was an odd pleasure to hear that although so much had changed, so much hadn't.

Frank knew that if he complained long enough Bob

would eventually surrender a bit of ancient wisdom that would save him countless hours and headaches. On occasion, he would bring by a set of blueprints for Bob to look at and suggest how to get around certain problems. Other times, if he framed his dilemma in just the right way, he'd even convince the old man to come by and help. Bob was Frank's guru. Frank, on the other hand, was Bob's excuse to take a break, have a beer, and chat.

After twenty minutes or so, the younger man decided he had taken enough time away from Bob's cabinet making and rose to leave. Watching Bob pull his feet off of his makeshift stool, Frank thought he might scratch an itch of curiosity. He casually asked, "So, Bobby, whatcha using for a foot rest there?"

Bob thought for a moment. He then slowly leaned forward and lovingly pulled the sheet back. He looked up at Frank with a sly smile and asked, "What do you think it is?"

"A rock?" said Frank whose face couldn't help but show disappointment.

"Try to pick it up," the old man challenged.

Frank bent down, wrapped his arms around the small, blackened boulder and heaved. It didn't budge. It was as though it was glued to the garage floor. Frank looked up at Bob in pained fascination.

"Bobby, what in the *hell* do you have here?"

Bob got up, walked to the cooler and pulled out two more beers. He then returned to his seat and asked, "You got time for a story, Hillbilly?"

Frank sat back down in his lawn chair and stared bewildered at what was clearly not just a rock.

"About fifteen years ago my brother and I, along with a few others, would take a yearly fishing trip up to Quebec and the lakes around the Hudson Bay. Now, three hundred miles into Quebec is no man's land, Hillbilly. It's pure wilderness. It's just you, the lakes, a whole lot of fish, and hopefully not too many bears. Anyhow, it's a fisherman's paradise up there.

"Well, you probably already know that fishermen are kinda territorial. So to avoid giving away the best fishing spots, they have a code by which they navigate all these uncharted islands and talk about their favorite holes to one another. They'll say, 'We caught such and such at Sailboat Island,' or 'We caught this big one over at 'Bill's Bar & Grill.'

"One year, near the end of our trip, we'd been fishing all morning and decided to take a lunch break on Burnt Island. The story went that the island had burned to the ground about forty years ago, hence the name. The Indians in that area claimed it had been struck by lightning. So we decided to pull up to it, have lunch, and bathe while we were there. We always bathed in the lakes.

"So here we were, four grown men running around this island, bare-naked after a sobering cold bath, drying off in the sun, and having lunch. Well, as fortune would have it, *nature called*. I had to go offload a few of the beverages I'd been drinking. Anyway, I'm standing there, doing my business, when I see this rock lying nearby. It looked like a briquette out of a barbeque grill. I didn't think much about it until I noticed that it was the only briquette around. It was completely different than any of the other rocks on

158

the island. I called my brother over and asked him what he made of it. He said it was just a rock and the other guys agreed. They didn't seem to be all that impressed with it. But it was definitely out of place, which intrigued me. There were small pieces of it lying around, so I grabbed a few of them and stuffed them in my bag. I also took real close and detailed pictures of it. The rest of the guys thought I was nuts. Long story short, we left the island, finished out the week, and came home.

"Well, when I came home, I couldn't stop thinking about that rock up on Burnt Island. There wasn't much I could do about it for the time being since it was covered over by water now, frozen solid like an ice cube until next summer. But I just knew there was something odd about it, so I started doing some research. I was on the Internet every night. I got books and journals about geology and started getting pretty obsessed. I had always loved collecting rocks anyway, so this was right up my alley. And after a few months I had come to the crazy conclusion that that rock sitting up there, three hundred miles into nowhere, may just be some sort of meteorite.

"I took the pieces I had to all kinds of specialists, some famous, some not so famous. But most of them didn't have the time, money, or the interest to really give it a fair shake. When it came to discoveries, and being territorial, I quickly found that there was one species worse than fisherman – geologists. Most of the ones I talked to had no interest in it because they weren't the ones who had found the rock, nor did they see any way for them to profit from it.

"Finally, I took it to an expert geologist, suggested by

everyone who had seen it. I think his name was Whitfield. After studying it for a few minutes he looked at me and said, 'Mr. Darcy, I don't believe what you have here is actually a meteorite from outer space. Instead, what I believe you have found is something called a *terrestrial* meteorite. You see, about a billion years ago asteroids hit the earth while it was forming. When these asteroids, with their incredible size and speed, made impact upon the earth's crust, they dislodged pieces of the earth and sent them up into space. The same sort of thing happened with the moon. We know that asteroids hit the moon and sent pieces of it shooting into outer space, some of which happened to land here on the earth. Unfortunately, the pieces that are dislodged from the earth by asteroids rarely find their way back down to earth. However they do, on occasion, 'come home.' Look at these pieces Mr. Darcy. The outside of them has been super-heated, almost like someone fired them with a blowtorch. We call that the fusion crust. At the core of these small samples alone I can make out amethyst, ruby, flecks of gold, silver and other precious gems. A conglomeration of these materials in one specimen points to something extremely unusual. These ancient wonders are so rare, we have very little to compare them to. Many even disbelieve there are samples large enough for them to evaluate. And you say you've found a specimen approximately two feet in diameter? Extraordinary! If what you claim is true Mr. Darcy, its value is, well, rather substantial... possibly even incalculable...'

"Needless to say I was pretty excited about what I heard. So I spent the whole next year researching. And the more I learned, the more I became convinced that Whitfield was right. Now I just had to get this rock that had come back down to *its* home back to *my* home.

"My brother and I spent a lot of time that year devising a way to bring the rock back. We kept it hush-hush though. We didn't want to blab to the wrong person and find our rock gone by the time we returned or get stopped by the border patrol to have it confiscated. It certainly wasn't illegal to bring home rocks. We'd always brought rocks home from Canada for fire pits or to line gardens. But we'd never brought back something so valuable or heavy. Why, just getting it off the island into a small fishing boat would be tricky. As you just found out Hillbilly, that rock weighs close to four hundred pounds.

"I spent many a night lying awake in bed, pondering how to bring it back. Eventually, I had a piece of canvas made into a circle with leather straps around the outside of it so that four or five men could stand around and lift it. Then, come August, we loaded up the trucks and fishing boats and headed back up to Quebec, hopefully returning this time with not only a nice catch of fish, but also the greatest geological discovery of the twentieth century.

"Sure enough, when we returned to Burnt Island, there it sat. As I stood and looked at it, I couldn't help but tear up a little. After a whole year of research, study, and sleepless nights, here it was - just the way I had left it. I scanned the island again and searched for a few more clues. There was no other rock that even compared with the one I had found. What's more, all the growth seemed new. The trees there on "Burnt" Island were much smaller than anything else we were used to seeing up there. I just knew we were onto something special.

"But we didn't have time to fool around. Dark clouds were coming up in the west. We needed to get the rock back to camp before the water got too rough to transport it. The last thing we needed in the bow of the boat during a strong thunderstorm was a four hundred pound rock. We'd be swimming in no time with my prize making its way to the bottom of the lake.

"We stood around the rock, rolled it onto the canvas, and the five of us carefully hoisted it into the front of the boat. Just as we set it down, the first drops began to fall. It was a thirty-minute trip back to camp. For precaution, I had wrapped a tether line around it with a hundred feet of rope attached to a float just in case something happened. Within ten minutes, the wind had picked up and the water got real choppy. The rain started coming down in buckets. The boat was rocking like a kid's toy in a bathtub. I crawled up to the bow and wrapped myself around that rock like it was a life preserver. Everyone was laughing at me, but if that rock went over, I was going with it. I was going all the way to the bottom if I had to!

"Well, finally we reached our campsite, soaked to the bone but glad our prize was still with us. We took our gear out of the boat, left the rock inside, and hoisted the boat up into the back of the truck. And there it sat for the rest of the week until we left. We also collected a few other rocks to put around the meteorite so that, to the border patrol, it would look like just another rock we were bringing back.

"You have never seen two happier people than when my brother and I finally made it back over the border. The patrol stopped us like they did every truck coming and going.

We almost messed our pants when they checked the back of the truck and took a look inside the fishing boat. We just sat quiet in the cab, held our breath, and prayed that border cop wasn't an expert on terrestrial meteorites. Boy, we must have looked like two cats that had just swallowed the canary when he came around to the cab to speak to us.

"Thanks for visiting Canada, move along..."

About five miles past the border, we wheeled into a truck stop, pulled a couple of beers out of the cooler, and had ourselves a little party. The rock was finally ours.

"When we first got home, we spent a lot of time talkin' about what we would do with the millions of dollars we'd make. We had dreamed for a whole year about what the rock could be and how we'd bring it home, but we didn't plan for what happened next, which was...well, nothin'."

Frank stared back at Bob in confusion.

"Whatdaya mean nothing?" Frank said like a child who didn't get to finish his bedtime story.

"Well..." Bob continued, "Nobody wanted it. Or at least nobody wanted to believe that an ol' boy who swung a hammer for a living had found something so important. We called and contacted geologists and museums of all sorts and stripes. They said we'd have to go through a process by which the rock would need to be 'authenticated,' meaning years and years of research trying to disprove it so they could eventually prove it. Basically they told us, in no uncertain terms, that they'd just give us the run around until we gave up trying. Either that or they claimed that they just didn't have the time to help us. In the end it would have cost a fortune just to convince someone to take me seriously. So here it sits." Bob looked down at the rock and smiled like a proud father. "Beautiful isn't it?"

He held out a small piece of the rock lying by the larger one that had its core exposed. Frank took it, held it up to the light and goggled.

"Wow...that is gorgeous! So let me get this straight..." he said, handing the weighty piece back to Bob. "You have a rare meteorite, possibly worth millions of dollars and significantly important to science that nobody has the time to look at, just sitting here in your shop that you use as a footrest?"

"Well Hillbilly, it is what it is," said Bob with a slight smile that conveyed his acceptance. "Oh, I figure one day someone will come along - someone who realizes what it is and what it's worth. Maybe they'll even be able to do something with it, but I'll be long gone by then. The point is, I know what it is. *I* know what it's worth. I look at it every day when I come out here. It makes me laugh to think about what I did to get it. The thought that one day, someone is going to get the surprise of their life in this old work shop makes me hope that God lets me look down from heaven, just so I can see the look on their faces. Hey, that reminds me... You were lookin' for a wrench, ain't that right?" Bob covered the rock back up again and began looking around his shop. He walked over to a rusted toolbox lying underneath some yellowed newspaper, opened it, and produced a pipe wrench that nobody made anymore.

Brought back to the reason he had come in the first place, Frank marveled at the antique wrench and shook his head.

"Bobby, you never cease to amaze me. You got more tales and fun toys tucked away in this ol' garage than anyone would ever believe."

Bob just smiled and said, "Well Hillbilly, don't go tellin' everyone or they'll all be droppin' by to borrow stuff. And then I'll never get to finishing these cabinets for ol' lady Simms up the road."

Frank took the wrench, shook Bob's firm hand, and hopped back into his truck. Then he slowly headed out of the twisting driveway and turned on his radio. Playing on the station was a George Straight song he hadn't heard in ten years.

As he made his way over the rolling hills that led him back to his home in Delta, Frank wondered if Bobby's rock would ever be discovered - if someone who had the knowledge and the means would eventually come along, realize its value, and share it with the world.

The cool breeze blowing through his open window put Frank in a reflective mood. It struck him that you never know what you'll find when you look under the sheet. Amazing what you'd learn if you spent enough time with a good friend. Old songs and garages, burnt rocks and beers sometimes contained rare gems, like the autumn leaves that swirled in the road wind as he made his way home.

The Suitcase

As the story goes, Bill Mitchell was not a notable man. He was not a rich man or a poor man. He was not a famous man or an important man. He was not a good man or a bad man. He was just a man. Blessed with a family, two kids and a wife, he worked as a produce manager at the local grocery store every day, from five-thirty in the morning to four in the afternoon. His weekends were a mix of kids' soccer games, mowing the lawn, church on Sunday, and maybe cooking out on the grill if the weather was nice. A more pedestrian existence would be difficult to imagine.

But that all changed one morning in late May when Bill finally got around to starting a small vegetable garden in his backyard. He and Sue had never attempted a garden, but with the rising cost of groceries, they figured a few home-grown tomatoes and peppers might be worth a shot. Bill had never dug a real garden, so what happened may have been the result of his inexperience. He could have started digging up the lawn in too wide a swath, or maybe he dug too deep. Gardening skills aside however, one thing is for certain: he struck gold, literally.

It is now the stuff of legend the way Bill's shovel happened to hit something hard while working that morning. After a half-day's work, his back was just about to give out.

Whatever he hit, it definitely was not a rock. Bill was quite familiar with that sound by now. The mysterious obstacle had piqued his interest, so he ignored the ache in his back and the rising blisters on his hands and continued to dig. Finally, he was able to get his shovel underneath the stubborn object and pop it out of the ground. It seemed that what he had spent his whole morning digging up was a suitcase: a suitcase full of money - ten million dollars in cash to be exact. There was no telling where it had come from or how it got there. The only hint of its origin was an engraving on the handle of the suitcase itself. It simply read, **S. N. Joy.**

Needless to say, Bill didn't go to work the next morning...

From that fateful moment on, life changed fairly rapidly for the Mitchell family. They moved into a new house - not a mansion, but big enough. Sue could finally quit her job at the bank. The kids didn't have to worry about college, nor would their children's children for that matter. Little Abby could finally get those braces she needed. And suddenly, the biggest thing Bill had to worry about was whether his tee-time would conflict with his time spent lounging by the pool or fishing in his new boat.

Then one day, in the middle of a hot August afternoon, the doorbell rang. Bill was just about to fix himself a sandwich when he went to open the door to find the oddest-looking individual he'd ever seen. Standing there was an older man dressed in flip-flops and rolled up golf pants. Large sweat stains decorated a white and red flowered Hawaiian shirt. He had a salt and pepper mop of unruly hair and a dark tan hiding underneath his unshaven face. Ray

Ban sunglasses, circa 1985, completed the stranger's look as he stood like a melting snowman in the summer sun on Bill's front porch.

"Excuse me sir," he said, "I was just out for a little walk when I realized I'd forgotten just how hot a North Carolina summer day can get. Could I bother you for a glass of water?"

Feeling charitable, Bill invited the stranger in and quickly poured him a glass of cold water from the refrigerator door.

"Nice fridge!" the stranger commented.

"Yeah, it's amazing how big these things are and yet how little they actually can hold," Bill said jokingly.

The stranger just chuckled and helped himself to a seat on the Mitchell's brand new sofa.

Bill made himself comfortable in the chair facing the couch. He had a tee-time scheduled in an hour or so, but he figured he could spare a few moments for this obviously ill-prepared walker.

Bill shook the man's hand and introduced himself.

"Hi I'm Bill. I don't think I've ever seen you around here before…"

"Well," the stranger replied, "seeing that you just moved in a few months ago, you probably haven't. I reckon you'll get to know the lay of the land pretty soon. Actually, in a manner of speaking, you probably know me better than you think. You can call me Sam, but my given name is actually Samuel Norman Joy."

Bill felt his heart start to pound in his chest and

his mouth went dry. The stranger just looked at him with an innocent smile. S. N. Joy - the name on the suitcase. It couldn't be...

Bill stammered out a few words, but before he could say anything coherent, the stranger continued, "Yup, you got it. The initials on the suitcase; those are mine. I was wondering how long it would take someone to find it. I guess those cases are a lot more durable than I thought they'd be."

Bill began to speak, "Mr. Joy w-we tried to find the owner. We actually did a search... What did you say your name was again?"

But Sam continued like Bill hadn't said a word.

"Well Bill, aren't you going to show me around the place? This is a mighty fine house you've acquired here. And please don't call me Mr. Joy! That's my father's name. You can call me Sam."

Then Sam rose from the couch and started to amble through the house taking in everything with a smile on his face and a whistle on his lips. Meanwhile, Bill Mitchell was right on his heels asking about lawyers, lawsuits, and statutes of limitations on finding a suitcase full of someone else's money, all of which Sam Joy ignored entirely. The stranger paused to look into the kids' rooms. He smiled at Sue as she carried a load of laundry down the hall. He even sauntered into Bill's new office, sat behind his desk, and took a twirl or two in the overstuffed leather chair.

When Sam had completed his tour of the house, he came back into the main living room and flopped back down on the sofa like he'd lived there his entire life. Bill came running in after him and sat across from him.

"Listen Mr. Joy... I mean Sam. I'm sure this is not what you expected to find, and I'm sure your lawyers will be contacting me very shortly. You must know we tried everything we could to find you, to give you back your money. I can't say how terribly sorry I am..."

Sam cut him off.

"Bill, I didn't come here to put you in such a tizzy. If I had known you'd get all upset, I'd have just sent a letter. Who said anything about lawyers or lawsuits? You need to relax, son. I'm not here to take any of this away from you. As a matter of fact, I'm honestly proud of all you've done here. Your wife looks happy. Your kids look well taken care of. You've obviously made some good choices with your discovery. I'm happy for ya."

"Mr. Joy, I don't understand..." said Bill bewilderedly.

"You see Bill," Sam continued, "I come from money... more money than any man could possibly spend in a hundred lifetimes. Fortunately, I realized a long time ago that to share what I had would actually bring me the greatest amount of pleasure in life. So, I decided to start giving it away. But I didn't want to do it the way everyone else goes about giving away money, not with the tax and charitable giving laws being what they are. Instead, I came up with my own creative way to share the wealth - the ol' suitcase method... Clever, huh?"

"But Sam," said Bill, "I don't understand. Why me? Why us?"

"Now Bill, you don't think you're the *only one* I've left a suitcase for, do ya? But, I'm glad you're the one who found that particular case, and I couldn't be more delighted to see that you and your family are doing so well!"

With that, Sam rose from the couch and walked toward the front door. Bill chased after him and grabbed him by the arm.

"Thank you Sam."

"You're very welcome, son."

Sam opened the door and began walking down the driveway. But just as he came to the street, he turned and yelled back up the driveway to Bill who was standing at the door.

"William Mitchell, are you enjoying my money?"

Bill yelled back with tears in his eyes.

"Yes sir. Yes I am. Yes *we* are!"

"Good! That's very good!" Sam yelled back.

And then, Samuel N Joy smiled, turned, and with a whistle, walked down the street, disappearing as he rounded the corner.

Sparrow,

Now that you have come to the end, maybe you have come to a new beginning as well. Of course all the work of change is left to the Divine Spirit to move in each of us in her own way. Give her space. Give her time. Give her the freedom to show you your own place in each tale. If there is chaff, let it be blown away. If there is gold and silver to be had let it be stored in your heart like treasure and given out to those who need it most, in due season.

F.T. is assumed to be no longer, and it is said that his work is finished in this world. But I assure you, he is still very much among the living and, as always, seeking out the company of inquisitive brothers and sisters to share with (especially if there is a pint involved in the transaction). The likes of Emeeca, Captain Ultra, and Hogard the mighty giant still live on as their stories grow and their adventures teach them new lessons.

Perhaps someday you and I will have the pleasure to meet. Until then, be assured that although there is terrible mischief and trouble still at work in our world, a great light has come! Although our own blindness leads us to some of the most wretched places, ultimately nothing can undo the great stroke of love that has smitten sin and death – the great, great love of our Father, in whose arms we all abide and one day will see face to face.

You too have been included in the Great Embrace… Awaken and enjoy!

Friar Tuck

Acknowledgments

I absolutely could not have written this book without the love and support of my wife Amy, and my kids. The adventure we live as a family constantly amazes me and I couldn't ask for more splendid traveling companions.
I love you all.

I am also indebted to Elizabeth Liskey and especially Robin Seiple, both admitted grammar police, who happily took on the task of cleaning up my mess, copy editing, critiquing, and gently guiding me in the ways of the semicolon.
Thank you ladies!

My very cool sister Chelsea Heilman designed the cover. What's more, when it became clear I needed help beyond my expertise she graciously lent her hand to the layout of the final manuscript.
Oh the depth of a sister's love!
Thank you Chelsea.

Countless friends and family encouraged me to FINISH THE BOOK when I wanted to quit: Dad, Curtis, Rhonda, Thomas, Ernie, John, and many others...
In the words of that great poet Rocky Balboa
"YO ARDIAN, I DID IT!!!"

Acknowledgments Cont...

Finally, I'd like to thank Dr. Baxter Kruger,
brilliant theologian and friend, for absolutely ruining my life
in the best way possible. By him, over a pint in a tiny bar in
Norfolk, I was unceremoniously ripped out of the matrix of
religion and introduced to the larger world I'm now
learning to swim in.

In this world Jesus reigns as all and all.
Everything else is a happy footnote, gladly embraced by the
Triune God of Grace who has included hopeless sinners,
beggars, thieves, and common outlaws (as well as the rest of
the cosmos) in his embrace. This is the reality I have come
to know and have been blessed to share with you.

J.H.

Joe Heilman is a native of Baltimore, Maryland who tells crazy stories, writes and sings decent songs, hangs out in shady bars and churches, really loves his wife and kids, and enjoys taking long walks with his dog.

Printed in the USA
CPSIA information can be obtained
at www.ICGtesting.com
CBHW021237180724
11790CB00009B/329

9 780615 571430